TELL ME YOUR
SWEET LIES

Gio Gregory & Ken Gregory

ISBN: 978-1-65909-080-2

Also available as on eBook

DEDICATION

Gio Gregory 7 Oct. 1956 – 10 Sept. 2019

This novel is dedicated to the memory of my darling wife and co-author, Gio Gregory. It was whilst we were editing the book in Paimpol, Brittany that she became unexpectedly ill and unbeknown to us at the time, had suffered a Deep Vein Thrombosis in her leg. The resulting blood clot travelled to her lungs to cause a Pulmonary Embolism. This is an extremely serious and potentially fatal condition, and so it proved to be in my darling Gio's case despite battling bravely for 5 days in an induced coma.

III

I would also like to dedicate this work to the people of Brittany who were so kind and helpful to my daughters and I, the valiant medical staff of the Centre Hospitalier de Saint Brieuc, who gave her the best possible care and the wonderful volunteers of the Maison des Famillies de Patients Hospitalisés who made sure we could stay close by during that time.

Gio passed away on the morning of what would have been our 42nd wedding anniversary. I will miss her every minute of every day.

All proceeds from the sale of this book will be donated to the charity Thrombosis UK, whose mission is to improve the prevention of venous thromboembolism and ensure everyone recognises the signs and symptoms of Deep Vein Thrombosis and Pulmonary Embolism.

Visit: - thrombosisuk.org

PROLOGUE

'Here boy, come here Merlin,' the dog walker's voice commanded. The dog shows no interest in obeying its owner's demands, it's more interested in sniffing at what looks like a homeless person lying on the muddy riverbank. Merlin eventually looks up at its master's repeated requests but continues sniffing at the slumped body on the ground.

The dog's master sighs. He doesn't have time for this. Just 30 minutes to walk the dog, get home, get showered and head off to work is a tight time schedule as it is and he doesn't need this, not today of all days. The man doesn't understand why Merlin won't come to heal and now he's looking up at his master and barking... as if he's saying, 'come here and look at this.'

The dried, stony riverbank uneven under his feet causes the man to stumble and quicken pace yet he recovers as he hears Merlin whimpering at the limp body lying motionless on the low tide mud of the River Thames. On approach he sees the form is a man, not a young man, motionless. His overcoat drenched in water, his head face down on the ground. By the look of his shrivelled hands it's obvious he's been in the water for some time.

Grabbing Merlin's collar to draw the dog to his side, patting his flanks to sooth the troubled animal, the man tries to waken the body by touching his lifeless shoulder. He knows there's no point in doing this but he tries it anyway hoping a miracle will happen.

'Hey, how are you doing matey?' He asks the lifeless body. There is no response. He didn't really expect one. No miracles today.

The police arrive quickly, followed just 4 minutes later by an ambulance. Merlin and his owner sit on a bench nearby and answer a few questions the police officer asks him. When did he find the body? What time did he leave the house? That sort of thing. The man has never seen a dead body before and he realises that maybe his plans for the day weren't that important after all.

At the inquest the coroner describes the results of the autopsy. The cause of death of the man, a white male aged 58 who was identified from the driving license in his sodden jacket, was drowning. But there were other unexplained matters that caused the coroner some concern. It was true the body contained excessive amounts of alcohol, but there was extensive bruising to the man's torso and other contusions to the arms, as if force was used to hold the man. The family could throw no light on any possible reason for such an awful tragedy to occur. He was a well-liked, respected professional with a loving family. His daughter had flown in from New York, where she lived and worked, to be there at the inquest and to support her mother who sat through the proceedings, seemingly unable to comprehend what had happened. The coroner recorded an *Open Verdict*, with a request to anyone who had witnessed anything, or who had any further information which might help the case, to come forward.

PART 1

CHAPTER 1

I can't remember when it was exactly that I realised Oliver was not the one. All I know is that every little thing he does seems to annoy me now. I had thought we had lots in common, but one by one those little things began to irritate me. So much so, that now those little things are just one big annoying thing… him.

Oliver is just not what I am looking for in a man and I could kick myself for allowing things to get so far and right now he's really getting on my nerves. If he doesn't stop this minute, I will explode. I'm desperately trying to concentrate but he insists on standing behind me as I sit at my desk attempting to massage the knots in my tense neck and shoulders and I wish he'd stop as he's really not very good at it. I wish he wasn't touching me at all.

'Lucy' I called to my assistant, who was straightening some of the pictures on the gallery wall. 'I'm just going into the back office to put these things back in the safe.'

'Oh, I'll come with you then,' Oliver chips in, uninvited. 'You know that I'd just like a quick peak at it again,' he continues in a mock whisper, loud enough for Lucy to hear as well.

I notice how she gives him one of her scathing looks of disgust. She's never said anything, but I knew she did not like Oliver one little bit.

He follows me as I pick up a pile of documents, rise from my chair and walk to the door marked

Private. Oliver is close behind and although I'd prefer some privacy at least, mercifully, he's not digging his thumbs into the back of my neck anymore.

The safe in my private office is embedded in a wall behind a black-and-white photograph of my late grandparents, Sam and Lucia Harper. As I swing aside the photograph I could feel Oliver's eyes practically burning in to the back of my head, I just knew he was trying to catch a glimpse of the numbers I was selecting on the combination lock of the safe. I shielded my actions so he could not see. That's another thing, he's so bloody nosey.

After placing the documents in the safe, I withdrew the battered, flat cardboard box from its resting place which I knew Oliver was interested in, pulling onto my hands the white cotton gloves reserved for handling objects of age or value, possibly both. Carefully lifting the lid from the box, Oliver leaned over my shoulder to get a closer look. I turned my head to look at him with an expression that said, *back off*. He understood and took a step back.

Now I had the space I needed, without the feeling of him breathing down my neck, I lifted out the slim, tissue bound package contained within the box and placing it upon the desk, unfolded the covering with reverent care to reveal the drawing that Oliver was so desperate to see.

'I know I've said this a thousand times Rebecca,' Oliver muttered in awe, staring at the artwork, 'but I'll say it again. I'm convinced this is an original.'

'Maybe it is, maybe it isn't,' I replied. 'But as I've told you a thousand times in return, I'm not interested in finding out. It stays here in the safe.' I covered the drawing up again, deciding that I had let Oliver see the ancient sketch for long enough.

'Well you know what I think. It's a shame you won't allow to get it properly appraised so that you'd know once and for all. If it is, as I suspect, an original Michelangelo then it's worth millions Rebecca, actual millions of pounds, dollars, yen whatever you want. You'd never have to work a day of your life again.'

I laughed at his suggestion. 'Will you give it up Oliver,' there he was, being all annoying again. 'You know that I think it's no such thing.'

I wasn't going to elaborate on my opinion, why should I have to justify myself to anyone, let alone Oliver? Again, I could kick myself. Why I had ever shown him the drawing in the first place I don't know, but what surprised me next was that he just shrugged his shoulders as though at last, after months of him pestering me, he had accepted my view that it was just a random old drawing that the family had owned for a couple of generations. It's nothing special, just an old drawing. Maybe I have worn him down at last?

Now all I needed to do was to tell him that I think we should end our relationship. Of course we could still be friends, I'd suggest. Oh God, what a cliché. Do people actually say that when they break up?

'Anyway,' Oliver announced, 'I was wondering if you'd like to go out for dinner this evening?'

'Err, yes I'd like to,' I answered automatically. As soon as I said it, I wish I hadn't. What was wrong with me, why couldn't I tell him exactly how I felt?

That's great, how about I meet you at Nico's at 7.30? I'll make a reservation and just to whet your appetite, I've got something special for you which I'm sure you'll love. Gotta run now, I've an appointment across town and I don't want to be late.'

And with that, plus a quick peck on the cheek, he was gone.

That was weird, I'd never seen him just shrug off a discussion about the drawing so nonchalantly before. Yes, I'm definitely wearing him down. All I need to do now is find the right time to let him all the way down, gently of course.

But I'm worried now about his motives for this evenings dinner date. I wonder what the *something special* that he says he has for me is. It couldn't be an engagement ring, could it? Of course it couldn't and I dismiss the idea, although of course we have sort of been here before.

I uncover the drawing once more to take a look myself. I'm pretty sure I know what the significance of this piece is. After all, I ought to know as 16th century Italian Art is supposed to be my speciality, particularly so as I spent a year obtaining my 1st in Art History in Rome. But maybe I prefer not to know and open up a can of worms about why the family has been in possession of it for so long; keeping it hidden. Once again, I could kick myself. What had I been thinking when I showed Oliver? I suppose I was trying to impress him after I had taken ownership of the gallery. We bumped into each other again quite by accident when I was working for Sotheby's in New York. He had flown over for an auction of Impressionist work, which was his area of particular interest, and as two old friends alone in a foreign country we went out for dinner that evening to catch up.

We had first met at University back home in England where we were born studying Art History. Actually, I was smarter than Oliver as I was studying Art History and Italian whilst he could only manage the history bit. But in fairness, Italian came easily to me as my grandma Caterina, or Nonna as I called her, was Italian. She met my grandfather during the war when he was with the allied forces who had swept north through the country, chasing the Nazis back home.

Oliver and I sort of dated on and off for a while during my final year at Uni in England and to be fair he helped me through a difficult time. But then I returned to Rome to do my Masters and although I promised to stay in touch, I didn't. There were just too many distractions in the eternal city to think about him in England.

I did come home to England though after completing my studies in Italy where I got my first job at the National Gallery in London. I enjoyed my three years there until I moved to Sotheby's where after a further three years I transferred to their New York offices. All that time back in London, actively working in the world of Art and I never bumped into Oliver once. I moved to New York and hey presto I bumped into him there. What's the chance of that? And then Poppa's tragic and untimely death meant I came home to London.

It never occurred to me that I would take over the family business and start running the gallery quite so soon. Sure it was always going to happen I suppose, but I hadn't thought it would happen so quickly and I was enjoying my life up until then. Rome, London, New York, but I was surprised how much I enjoyed working for myself. Then of course as Oliver and I had got back together again in New York, it seemed logical to keep seeing each other in London, especially during that sad time for us when he had been supportive and his support had led me to show him the drawing.

I wrapped it back up, placed it back in the safe where it should have remained all the time.

I needed to think what to wear for dinner this evening. What do you wear for a break-up meal?

Lucy glared at me as I stepped back into the gallery. 'Listen,' she said. 'I know it's none of my business Rebecca but I've got to say something.'

'What's that?' I asked.

'You can do so much better than Oliver. He is not the man for you.'

'Actually, I've come to that conclusion myself Lucy, but I don't quite know how to tell him. He's been so kind in the past and it feels wrong, sort of. What do I say?' I said to her in reply.

'Just tell him, come right out with it. Say… "Oliver, you're an idiot. I can do so much better than you and men are queuing up around the block to go out with me. Don't take it personally, but it's over." That should do it.'

'I can't say that,' I protested.

'Why not? It's always worked for me.'

I love Lucy, bless her. She was a godsend when Poppa died and I came back from New York. She kept the gallery running whilst we attended to everything that needed attending to. I don't know what we would have done without her to be honest.

She had worked for my father at the gallery for as long as I could remember and there were times when he got so exasperated with her he said he would give her the sack. But he would never have managed on his own without her being there and always seemed to forgive her for her outburst of blunt honesty. I remember Poppa telling me one time how Lucy had got so wound up with some pretentious, potential big spender that she told him he didn't know his arse from his elbow when it came to art and to get out of the gallery. But then another time she followed and harassed a mild-mannered couple, who had only come in to browse, for so long that the only way they could escape was to pay way over the odds for a piece of work they didn't even like.

13

I believe she was married once, a long time ago, but he didn't last the course. It was over within 6 months so I was told. Lucy was a woman who knew her own mind and what Lucy wanted, Lucy got. Despite being in her late fifties (none of us really knew her actual age as we were too afraid to ask) she still had an eye for the men. But none of those men could last the course either. They were a disposable item to Lucy.

'I'm going out for dinner with him tonight,' I told her, 'and I'm dreading it. I think he's going to propose.'

'Excellent,' said Lucy

'What do you mean, excellent?' I asked confused.

'Well, you just tell him no and to bugger off, job done.'

If only it were that easy, I thought.

***

In my opinion *Cuore Rosso* was the best Italian restaurant in Fulham, perhaps the best in all of London, but I would say that given I had been eating there since I was a child with my family. Luigi, the owner and chef, could conjure up the most delicious dishes with the simplest of ingredients and just like the food, the restaurant decor was also unpretentious. A feast attained without a hint of a red-checked tablecloth or an old candle in a raffia-wrapped Chianti bottle.

14

When I stepped inside the cosy restaurant, Luigi spotted me from the open kitchen and rushed over to greet me.

'Ciao Luigi, it's good to see you again,' I said to him as he greeted me with a kiss on each cheek.

'It is always good to have you eat with us *cara mia*,' he replied practically squeezing the air from my lungs. He was always very physical, like every Italian male I have ever met.

'Is Oliver here yet, I think he should have reserved a table?'

'Si cara, this way.'

I followed Luigi to a table for two at the rear of the room and I could see Oliver was getting a head start as he was already seated and nursing a large whiskey, which I thought odd as he wasn't normally a Scotch drinker. That's ominous, I thought. Why does he need Dutch courage? He did at least attempt to stand up when he saw me, although he looked a little unsteady. This was not a good sign.

One of the best things about Luigi's menu is that it's never the same two days running. He chalks up on a blackboard what he has decided to cook that day. Whatever happened that evening I was determined to enjoy a good meal when I saw Luigi had managed to procure Zucchini flowers which would be stuffed with ricotta and basil then deep fried. I was going to have that despite the calorie counter racking up the points in my head and I would follow that up with Osso Bucco. I had read somewhere that red wine breaks down fat, so I also requested a bottle of Chianti to go with it. What's the point of going out to eat if you're not actually going to eat is what I say. I knew I would never be a super model anyway, so why starve yourself?

As always the food was excellent and I enjoyed every mouthful but there was something weird about Oliver's' demeanour. Usually you couldn't stop him talking, as he seems to have an opinion on everything, however this evening he was quieter than normal and seemed attentive to the things I had to say. Which was kind of refreshing on one hand but unnerving on the other to be honest. It was preventing me from enjoying things as throughout the meal I was thinking about the something special he had for me.

I thought the Chianti might help but Oliver was drinking more than his fair share of the bottle, and the Whiskey, so I was seriously considering asking Luigi for a second bottle when Oliver reached inside his jacket pocket and withdrew a white envelope.

'This is for you. It's the something special I said I wanted to give you.'

I took the envelope from him with surprise and a little relief, at least it wasn't a small box containing a ring, but I was curious what the envelope contained. Lifting open the unsealed flap along the envelope, I withdrew a glossy printed folder. On the front in bold red lettering was printed 'The Wellbeing & Physiotherapy Centre.'

'Open the folder,' Oliver instructed, suddenly animated.

Inside the folder was a printed card and written on that in equally bold letters were the words 'Gift Certificate' and under that in smaller lettering was 3 x Full Body Massage.

'Oh thanks Oliver, I could really use a massage', I replied thinking about the rough manhandling he had inflicted on my neck and shoulders earlier in the day. I slid the card back into its envelope. 'Now did you say you had something special to show me?'

'That's it,' he replied with the widest grin. 'It's my new business venture. The Wellness and Physiotherapy centre and you get to be its first client.'

So basically it was all about Oliver. He had been holding back on telling me he had another hair-brained scheme and he'd managed to make the supposed gift he had for me into an opportunity to talk about himself. In a way, I wasn't entirely surprised and this wasn't the first time he had embarked on one of his get rich schemes. I was sure this was just another one of them.

Before I had returned to London, and we had got together again, he'd invested in a restaurant specialising in Hungarian cuisine, despite never having been to Hungary or eaten any of the regions dishes. It closed after just three months. More recently he'd started an on-line travel agent for specialised luxury holidays that hadn't sent a single client anywhere. There were several similar clever ideas that Oliver had come up with over the past few years that he'd told me about

17

and all with the same level of success. Oliver couldn't help throwing good money after bad and for the life of me I couldn't understand why. He seemed to have a good life as an independent art appraiser but clearly that wasn't enough for him for some reason. I looked at the glossy wallet that contained my gift voucher and there was a photograph on the front of a very good looking man with his arms folded and a broad smile on his face.

'This is very nice of you Oliver but what do you know about wellbeing, and physiotherapy for that matter?'

'Enough to know that there's money in it. Wellness, mindfulness, exercise programmes, sports injuries, all that kind of stuff.'

Obviously he knew nothing about it and he'd just reeled off a load of unrelated words. I certainly wasn't convinced, so I removed the gift he had presented me with from out of the envelope again. 'Who's this guy in the photograph?' I asked, showing him the picture on the front of the wallet.

'That's Alex. I met him through a mutual friend and he's a fully qualified physiotherapist and sports injury expert. He's really keen on setting up in London and after I learned more about how good he is I thought I could help him out. There's good money in this sort of thing but he needed someone who knows London and an investor to get him set up and started.'

So the guy in the photograph was Oliver's new business partner and I had to admit he was very attractive. I wondered if the man in the photograph was for real or just a stock photo. Suddenly I was mildly curious. After all, what woman wouldn't be? Alex appeared to be an extremely attractive man.

'It's an interesting thing to get involved in Oliver, but are you sure about this? Have you done your homework this time?'

'Certainly I have,' he replied offended.

I still wasn't convinced. 'Hmm, but I haven't got a sports injury.'

'I know, look inside the wallet. Alex has many strings to his bow. He's very talented.'

Oliver took the wallet from me and opened it wide to display the text inside and handed it back to me. There in bullet points was a list of Alex's various talents. *Physiotherapy Sports Injury Care, Sports Massage, Deep Tissue Massage, Dietary Advice, Hypnotherapy.*

'Hypnotherapy too?' I asked.

'Yes, he's interested in the psychology of sportsmen and fixing minds as well as their bodies.'

I looked at the photograph again and thought about Alex's body then looked across at a semi-drunk Oliver sitting opposite and couldn't imagine two more different business partners and wondered how the two had met.

'I'd like you to meet him and let me know what you think,' Oliver added.

'Well, I'm flattered that you want my opinion,' I answered. 'But I'm not sure I'm qualified in this sort of thing to be much help.'

19

'No you are Rebecca, you are. You enjoy a massage and Alex is a very good on all levels. You don't need to be an injured footballer to benefit from his skills.'

I felt a warm flush go through me as he said that and the blood rush to my face, my heart skipping a beat. 'I don't know Oliver. I do like the occasional massage but usually from a female masseuse. I'm not sure it's appropriate being massaged by a male. Especially a full body massage.' I waved his gift certificate at him.

Oliver did the little boy who isn't getting his own way look, he was good at that as most men are, and slumped back in his seat. 'I hold up my hands and give up Rebecca, really I do. Why do I bother trying?'

I looked at pathetic little Oliver acting like a child across the table and then I looked once more at the photograph on the wallet maybe I could surrender to Alex's hands I thought secretly. I gazed at Oliver once more. I knew he most definitely isn't the one.

***

I didn't drive straight home after the meal, Oliver had found a new way to irritate me by acting like a child. I'd never understood why men, or one man in particular, felt that acting like a child is a way to get what you want. Perhaps he's still a mummy's boy, but I'm not his mummy and neither do I want to be. Ironically, I am driving south-west across the Thames on my way to

Richmond to see my mother, but girls talk to their mums for different reasons and I was going to talk to mine, not that she could listen.

The parking spaces at the Oaks Rest home were empty, so it was easy to get a spot close to the entrance. There weren't any defined visiting hours but strictly speaking, turning up at this time of night wasn't exactly normal, although I knew it would be okay. Pushing the button on the intercom to gain entry, the night receptionist recognised me and as the door locks buzzed, gestured me to step inside.

'Just thought, I'd sit with mum for a while if that's okay?' I asked, knowing there would be no objection.

'Sure, go ahead. She had a good day today, happy as a clam.'

'Thanks Annie, that's great. I'll be very quiet and promise not to wake her.'

Mum's room was on the first floor and I walked up to the stairs and along the corridor to her door on tip-toe. Slowly and carefully entering the room I closed the door gently behind me as I waited for my eyes to get used to the gloom, barely illuminated by the night-light. The figure in the bed was sleeping peacefully and now I could see my way, I walked silently over to her and sat in the chair next to her bed.

The Oaks Rest Home was absolutely the best place we were able to find to care for Alzheimer and Dementia sufferers. My brother and I had seen plenty that weren't good, believe me. The staff were all attentive and considerate and the resident's rooms tastefully furnished. I had made mum's room a little more comfortable by adding personal touches, such as a few family pictures and items from the old family home in an effort to make things a little more familiar for her.

As I sat in the chair next to her, I looked at mum sleeping peacefully and was grateful that for a few short hours at least, she would be untroubled. This was not how life was supposed to have panned out for her or for my father for that matter. First Poppa had been so cruelly taken away in the tragic drowning two years ago and then this dreadful, unforgiving condition had taken the mother I loved from her body and left an imposter in her place. An imposter who barely recognised me on the worst days. No, this was not what was supposed to happen. Life wasn't supposed to be like this.

When I went to New York, I did so reluctantly. Poppa was struggling with the gallery, business seemed slow and he seemed hesitant to share that with the rest of us. Then mum was beginning to show the early signs of her illness. But Poppa told me I couldn't put my life on hold and that I had my own life to lead. So I went to Sotheby's on a secondment and Poppa kept his secrets to himself.

You might think I came back to London to take over the gallery out of guilt and you'd be right. But in truth, I loved working there and running things. Although the jobs at the National Gallery and with Sotheby's had given me a good grounding in art and was fabulous experience, the gallery felt like home and I enjoyed the independence of it. Making my own decisions, knowing it was me I had to depend on to make a success of it and I was doing exactly that. It was very satisfying to find and nurture new artists, running exhibitions of their work and managing the sales, taking my ten percent of course. The aspect I enjoyed most, however, was seeking out pieces from the Old Masters hidden away in private collections, long since lost to public view. It was thrilling to find something of beauty locked away in some dusty old house after its owner passes away and the inheritor suddenly realises they have huge death taxes to pay. It was ironic really, death and art seemed to go hand in hand in my life.

I rubbed the aching muscles in my neck and shoulders and realised how tense I was, then remembered the envelope Oliver had given me in the restaurant. I searched for it in my handbag and opened it up again. The photo of the man on the cover looked back at me smiling. Was that actually the guy Oliver was going into business with or was he merely a model? He certainly could be, I thought. Good thick hair, strong jawline and a muscular body. He had his arms folded in front of him and I could tell this guy worked out. You could tell that by the definition of his chest underneath the tee-shirt he wore. I looked at mum again. Poor mum, life was just too short. The gift certificate slid out of the envelope and fell to the floor. I picked it up and looked at the bold words upon it. Three full body massages. Yes, I decided, life was too short not to.

CHAPTER 2

Oliver was uncharacteristically enthusiastic about me agreeing to see his attractive new business partner, which made me feel like I was sort of betraying his trust in me. He'd never really involved me in any of his previous get rich quick schemes so it felt like a small honour to be trusted in this way. He seemed genuinely interested to have my opinion and support but that only made me feel guilty as I was only really interested in meeting the Physiotherapist in the flesh. I was dying to see if it really was the man in the photograph and if it was, could he really be that attractive?

As Oliver drove us to the bar where he had agreed to meet, he chatted away about how he was sure this latest business venture was definitely the one that was going to work out this time.

'People are increasingly aware of health and well-being,' Oliver was expounding. 'So it stands to reason that they are willing to spend more of their disposable income on looking after themselves. Add to that the longer waiting times on the NHS for physio treatments, so the whole thing makes great business sense.'

I had to hand it to Oliver, he was really fired up about the imminent success that was coming his way, but then I remembered that although he hadn't ever consulted me in any of his prior attempts at entrepreneurship he was, as I recalled, equally excited about the Hungarian restaurant and the on-line travel agency.

Only this time he seemed to genuinely want my endorsement and approval. This turn of events was not how I had envisaged the past twenty-four hours panning out. Last evening at dinner I had fully expected that I would be ending things with Oliver and now here I was actively encouraging him. I tried to think about the number of reasons why I should break things off with him, the things that he did which annoyed me. But I looked at him now and he was happy and animated, just like a little boy. So I decided that would do for starters. I wanted a man, not a boy.

We made slow progress through the heavy evening traffic and I shifted uncomfortably in my seat, realising that the tension between my shoulders was still there. I remembered Oliver's unskilled attempt to massage knots in my neck and shoulder muscles. He really didn't know what he was doing, and I wondered if he really knew what he was doing this time too. I hoped he had teamed up with someone who was an expert. I couldn't bear the thought of some other man touching me in such a ham-fisted way. So I now had two reasons to end the relationship. Oliver was really just a boy and he didn't know how to touch a woman properly. There, I was getting somewhere now and I began to think of more reasons whilst Oliver prattled on about his vision for a chain of health and well-being centres across London and the South East.

The bar where we were due to meet was freshly refurbished in the style of a traditional country pub but failing miserably. Lots of shiny polished wood and stencilling on the walls promising Ales, Wine and Gin but at least the furniture looked comfortable, if not exactly traditional. We found a quiet corner to sit where Oliver could keep an eye on the entrance to watch for his new colleague.

Oliver went to the bar to buy us drinks and whilst he was there I took the envelope he had given me the night before from out of my handbag. I slid out the contents and looked again at the photograph on the front, realising now that I was nervous about meeting him but couldn't understand why. When Oliver returned with a large glass of Chardonnay for me he noticed that I was looking at the gift he had given me and once again started talking about his vision for the future but to be honest, I wasn't listening, just responding automatically with the occasional, *hmm, yes, really.* I was wondering what I was letting myself in for. Why hadn't I just told him things weren't working out for us, wish him well in his new venture and call it a day? Put an end to it. And then I saw him.

He stood framed in the doorway, scanning the room to spot Oliver. He had come dressed for business but not in the stuffy style his business partner wore. He sported tight skinny trousers, narrow at his ankles and his jacket was tailored to the right length not too long like most men wear. The sleeves hugged what I could tell were strong arms. He wore a smart white shirt with a cutaway collar, buttoned up at the neck with no tie. He was sex on legs.

Oliver saw him too and stood to wave him over to where we sat. I noticed other women look at him as he walked over to join us and for no reason I could think of, felt jealous because of it. The two men shook hands and then Oliver introduced me.

'Alex, this is my girlfriend Rebecca I was telling you about. Rebecca, meet Alex.'

'Girlfriend?' I said out loud in a shocked voice before I could stop myself. I had never considered myself to be Oliver's girlfriend. Not that it's in any way an old-fashioned sort of title and I don't actually believe it really is, despite the word falling out of favour. But didn't I want people to think of me as Oliver's girlfriend? He stared at me open-mouthed as though I was rejecting him and maybe subconsciously I was.

Alex could sense the sudden tension and the imaginary tumble weed rolling across the room. 'It's difficult these days to know what to call your significant other half isn't it? He interjected. 'And partner sounds like it's reserved for people with a mortgage and a joint bank account or people who are in business together. Anyway, I can see you're not a girl.'

Alex saved the day. I liked him immediately.

'I'll get us a drink shall I?' Asked Oliver, in a slightly grumpy tone.

'Lime and Soda water please Oliver,' replied Alex.

'Another large Chardonnay,' I added, only just realising I had already downed the first glass.

Oliver went to the bar and Alex reached out to shake my hand. His grip was oddly firm but gentle. He was attractive, very attractive and so different from Oliver in every way possible from the way he dressed to the way he smelt, oh and he smelt divine. I don't know what aftershave or cologne he was using, but it suited him. Alex was taller than Oliver, by a good two inches I'd say and his body well-toned without appearing overly muscular. He was certainly a bigger man than Oliver, I wondered if that meant everywhere? I flushed thinking about it.

'So Alex,' I said to cover my embarrassment and keep my mind on business matters. How did you come to meet up with Oliver?'

'Oh, through a mutual acquaintance,' He replied.

'In London?'

'No Cheshire.'

'Really, where abouts?'

'Near Wilmslow.'

For some reason he wasn't being particularly forthcoming with his answers. Perhaps he's a little shy, I thought, which would be a little awkward for a physiotherapist. Oliver returned with drinks and I downed the last drop in my glass before accepting a new one.

'So Alex tells me how you met each other up in Cheshire then Oliver,' I asked trying to get more beyond the short answers offered by Alex.

'Through a mutual acquaintance,' interrupted Alex as if to prompt Oliver.

'Yes, that's right,' Oliver agreed. 'I was up in Manchester doing some appraisals for a client who introduced me to Alex. I found out that he wanted to move his practice from Cheshire and set up in London. I saw it as a good business opportunity for both of us, so I offered to help and here we are.'

'I would have thought there was plenty of wealthy customers up in Cheshire to keep you busy Alex. Isn't Wilmslow in that area they call the Golden Triangle? Isn't that where all the rich footballers live?'

'The big clubs all have their own physios,' Alex explained. 'So I was always struggling to find enough clients.'

'There are richer pickings down here,' added Oliver. 'London's the place for a skilled man like Alex to make a name for himself.' He reached across the table and picked up the envelope he had presented me with over dinner… my special surprise.

'Look Alex,' Oliver continued excitedly. 'Here's the publicity stuff I got printed up and look at this gift certificate I gave to Rebecca.'

'You didn't really need to give Rebecca a gift certificate. If she's a friend of yours she just needs to come around to the office anytime she likes.' Alex responded.

30

I took the paperwork back from Oliver and opened the folder which gave details of the services offered by Alex. 'So what would you recommend?' I asked him. 'You seem to offer many services. Is that the right word… services?' My God, why did I say that? Services! I felt my face starting to flush again, but neither man seemed particularly phased by it.

'Well, I wouldn't imagine you need any physiotherapy,' Alex came back with. 'You look pretty fit to me.'

Now it was his turn with a less than subtle innuendo, I felt my face getting redder. Was he flirting with me now? Still, Oliver didn't seem perturbed at the way our conversation was heading.

'Alex is a trained hypnotherapist too Rebecca,' said Oliver.

'Maybe he'd like to get me under his spell?' I said, testing to see if we might continue with our suggestive talk.

'Actually I only use hypnotherapy as a complimentary tool, particularly with sports psychology.'

I took it that Alex's factual reply bought an end to that style of conversation and we weren't playing anymore.

Oliver, who hadn't seemed to notice that anything overtly mischievous was going on in the way Alex and I were talking to each other, carried on the conversation in a more dignified manner.

'Alex is highly trained in several therapy and relaxation techniques. Back up north, doctors recommended him to provide complimentary therapy along with their own medical care.'

'Really?' I asked and noticed how Alex looked oddly embarrassed at the way Oliver had tried to compliment him. Was there shyness about the man I wondered?

'Absolutely,' continued Oliver. 'I can say without a shadow of doubt, you'd be very safe in Alex's hands.'

'Oh yes… not too safe I hope, perhaps you can show me?' I laughed and started on my second large glass of Chardonnay.

Now it was Alex's turn to blush.

CHAPTER 3

I arranged for Lucy to close up the gallery and I went home early to change for my massage appointment with Alex, but what to wear?

How do you dress for a massage with a male masseuse, especially one as hot as Alex? I hadn't really thought of that when I agreed to do this last night at the bar. It all seemed a bit of flirtatious fun, or maybe it was the third glass of Chardonnay. Now the reality of it was I needed to be practically naked for this man to touch me. It sounds fine, in fact it sounded exciting when I said it out loud the day before but now I had time to think about it I was just a little nervous. I'd had plenty of massages before, but they had always been by a woman. A man was a different proposition, especially this man.

First things first however, I'd better smell nice and I take a shower before I decide on what clothes to wear. After my shower I apply as much bath products as possible. Chanel body cream and excessive amounts of the matching eau-de-parfum. Okay, so I know Chanel might be considered a little *old school* by some, but it's still my favourite.

The correct underwear is very important. I could have chosen my biggest, thickest pair of black knickers but if Alex saw them what would that say about me? I chose my matching Intimissimi Italian bra and pantie set, an attractive nude with matching organza lace edging. I didn't know whether I should dress formally or casually; I wanted to set the right impression. This wasn't a date, I told myself so I decided on casual. My Ralph Lauren jeans, shirt and the new blazer I had just bought with gold-embossed Ralph Lauren badge on the pocket. Normally I'd wear a thong with jeans but for today's activities, definitely not. Why is the correct underwear so hard to choose? I checked my bum in the mirror, hoping I couldn't see any VPL. My Brazil cut panties would have to do.

A deep breath and off I go for a massage with Alex. Sexy, hot, Alex. I tried not to think about him being so attractive but already the thought of those hands touching my body was awakening the butterflies in my stomach.

I decided to take an Uber to rendezvous with Alex at his new office. I wasn't sure if I'd be able to park easily and also I wasn't sure about controlling the car properly as the butterflies were now doing a war dance in my stomach.

The car dropped me off just off Putney High Street and looking at the address on my gift certificate I could see my destination was a shop between an Indian Restaurant and a place offering cosmetic dentistry. I checked the address again, comparing it with the number on the door. The door was freshly painted white, as was the window frame at the front of the building with a milky film applied to the glass on both the door and the shop window to ensure privacy. I pushed the door open and stepped inside. There, sitting at some sort of reception desk, was Alex.

I'm not sure why but I hadn't expected that he would be the first person I would see. He stood up to greet me.

'Hi Rebecca, welcome to the Physio and Wellness Centre,' he announced, spreading his arms out wide to present his new workplace to me.

'As you can see, it's a work in progress. There's still a little work to do until we open properly.'

It looked to me as though this shop had previously been a hairdresser. The room was square and along one wall was a long shelf unit with three tall mirrors equally spaced along it. It wasn't what I expected, although to be honest I wasn't sure what I was expecting when I had agreed to come.

'Err yes, it's nice,' I said unconvincingly looking around the room.

'It will be,' Alex told me. 'We'll make this room into a waiting area with a couple of nice sofas, some potted plants, that sort of thing. The consulting rooms are finished though and they're much nicer. Why don't you come through?' He prompted me.

Alex made sure the front door was closed and locked and I followed him through a door to the rear of the building. I felt a little apprehensive that I was now alone with a man I hardly knew, locked inside this building. My heart was beating like a drum whilst the butterflies continued their dance.

The room he led me to was windowless and brightly lit, all the walls painted white. It had the look of a clinic or doctor's surgery. There were two chairs on one side of the room and an examination table on the other side. The type you would certainly see at a surgery. There was a second door which, I guess, led off to another room.

'Take a seat.' Alex invited. 'If you can fill this in for me Rebecca and I'll just pop next door to get the room ready.'

I looked around the room. On the wall was a degree certificate from the University of Birmingham proudly displaying that Alexander Michael Lewis was awarded a degree, Bachelor of Science (Honours) in Physiotherapy. There were several other certificates I noticed. One from The Chartered Society of Physiotherapy and another was a diploma in Hypnotherapy. I turned my attention to the clipboard and started to tick each 'no' box for the long list of ailments and allergies listed there. I signed and dated at the foot of the form as requested and waited for Alex to return. Within a few minutes he re-entered the room where I sat and he took the clipboard from me, taking a seat opposite me at the desk whilst he scanned my completed form.

'Excellent,' he agreed. 'All very healthy and no medication.' He signed the form himself, very professional I thought and then looked me square in the eyes. 'What sort of pressure would you like your massage to be?' he asked.

'Firm.' I answered.

'Firm it is then. Let's go next door shall we?' Alex showed me into the room he had come from a few moments earlier.

This room was much smaller than the other, with lighting emanating from the edges of dark wooden panels set onto walls, complimented by fragrant candles flickering. Soft, meditation style music played, which gave the room a relaxing mood. I have to say that it impressed me. A massage table stood in the centre of the room, expertly made up with crisp white sheets, with one corner folded back ready for me to lie down.

'So I'll just leave you to get comfortable,' Alex explained. 'You can place your clothes on the chair here and just take off as much as you're comfortable with. You can leave your jeans on if you wish. I'll be back soon.' And with that he was gone.

This was it then. I was committed now, and I told myself and making sure the door was firmly closed, slipped my shoes off placing them under the chair Alex had showed me. I undressed quickly, not knowing how soon Alex would return and no, I had no intention of keeping my jeans on. Now down to my underwear, I sat on the edge of the massage table with my back to the door to remove my bra. Now I was worried, did I have any back-fat? I didn't want him to see any back-fat. Feeling as far as I could behind me, I checked for any plumpness. There was definitely a little, but maybe it would disappear when I lay down. At least I hoped it would. Sitting on the edge of the massage table and hoping no other errant mounds of fat were visible, I threw my bra onto the nearby chair only for it to miss and fall to the floor nearby. It would have to stay there, I wasn't about to walk across the room to retrieve it; I needed to get that sheet over me quickly. I lay with my face in the cradle listening to the music and watching the flickering tea-light that was floating in the bowl set underneath the table in my line of sight. After a little while there was a gentle knock at the door.

'Ready now?' Alex's muffled voice asked.

'Ready.' I replied.

I heard him enter the room from my position lying face down on the table and somehow I could sense that he had walked round to the chair to pick my bra from off the floor. That was embarrassing, not a good first impression to set, I thought. I could see the shadow he cast on the floor through the face cradle in the table as he moved closer to me and then I could see his feet as he stood close to me. My breathing should have been calm and steady but it was short and rapid, I was tense and not as relaxed as I would normally be when anticipating the soothing hands of the masseuse. Then the sheets covering me lifted and folded back to cover my bottom but leaving my back exposed. All that remained between my nakedness and Alex now, were those thin sheets and the material of my panties.

He moved from the table and I could hear the sounds of him applying liquid onto his hands. Now my anticipation was rising at the thought of him touching me. I was helpless as I lay there,

38

my breathing more like panting… and then he touched me.

His hands felt warm and comforting as he placed them in the middle of my back and I involuntarily held my breath. He moved his hands up my spine, on to my shoulders and down my sides. My skin turned to goose bumps almost immediately, his touch having an instant, magical effect on me. I relaxed into the table, closed my eyes and let out a long, noisy breath as my skin turned to normal. Yes, Alex was touching me and it transported me to a place of calm.

I'd had plenty of massages over the years, but this was different. It felt more intense but restful, his hands strong and yet soft. Even though I asked him to be firm, there was a gentleness as the palms of his hands and the tips of his fingers kneaded the muscles in my back and shoulder but at the end of each stroke his fingers would ever so gently glide teasingly over my skin.

He could feel the tension in my neck and shoulder muscles, the knots within, then under my shoulder blades and suddenly the gentleness ended. I could feel him place his forearms upon my back and press his whole weight down on me. The change in his treatment surprised me and practically forced all the air from my lungs. But I felt a strange intimacy in this new technique, I wanted to feel the whole weight of him on me. Then I could feel his elbows following the curve of my shoulder blades, digging into my flesh. It hurt, but it hurt just enough. I was torn between pleasure and pain; it was as if Alex knew how much I could bear, how much I could stand without crying out. Expertly he worked the tension free, unknotting each muscle one by one. As he worked his magic upon my back, knowing the pain he was inflicting on me, Ales stopped at just the right moment then laid his hands flat on me for a few seconds as if to comfort and reassure me.

Soothingly his hands followed the shape of my shoulders and down my arms, his fingers briefly touching mine at the end of the movement. Oh, how I wished he had lingered there and our fingers had touched each other's for longer. I didn't want this to end, and it didn't. He continued to seek out each tight muscle in my back and caressed each one into submission. This was more than a massage. What we were doing was sensual, erotic. Yes, that was the word… erotic, and I knew now what I wanted. I wanted him on top of me, naked. His hands sent shivers right down my spine again and again as I thought about the prospect of Alex and me naked together, then for the second time my skin turned to goose bumps. Oh God, he must know what I was thinking, surely? Alex was so experienced in his art so surely he must know what turns a woman's skin so?

He knew because he folded the sheets back just below the waistband of my panties to expose the crease in my bottom and started to massage the base of my spine, gently at first and then firmly. He was manipulating me, oh so close to my lady parts. So close that he was arousing me.

What was he doing now though? He had stopped touching me and was moving away. I didn't want him to stop. Surely it wasn't time for him to stop? But no, he would not stop because after all my gift certificate specified a full body massage and Alex was folding the sheets away from my feet and legs, arranging them in a narrow band across my bottom so I was now ninety percent exposed to him. The only men who I'd ever revealed so much flesh to were my doctor, my mother and the few boyfriends I'd had. That included Oliver, and I tried to erase him from my mind as I suddenly knew that I had allowed someone who I now despised to see me naked, to see me so exposed and vulnerable. I wouldn't allow him to make me feel like that again, I vowed as I lay there for Alex; I wanted to be reckless with him. I wanted Alex to see me naked, all of me. Oh, those hands.

Those hands were now sliding up my calf muscles, slowly, rhythmically and then he took one of my feet in his hands, lifting it from the table and began to softly rub the soles of my foot with his thumbs. I would normally be super ticklish and not allow anybody to touch my sensitive feet, but he knew what he was doing and expertly soothed my aching feet, his thumbs making gentle circles in the arches. And now his hands were reaching further up my legs and just when I was willing him to go further… he stopped and pulled the sheets back over my legs again. What he did next was almost like sex. He gently traced his finger lightly from the nape of my neck

41

to the base of my spine sending a wave of delicious tingles through my body and then he covered me over with the sheets and a blanket. I could feel his two hands just lying flat and still on my back as though he was putting me to bed, preventing me from rising.

'Lie still until you're ready to get up,' he whispered to me. 'There's no rush at all. I have left some water for you and you can get dressed and come through to the other room when you're ready.'

With that he left me to myself. I lay there savouring the stillness and the warm glow that was rippling through my body. I didn't know how long the massage had lasted, but however long it was, it wasn't long enough. So I lay for a long time deep in my own thoughts about this man called Alex and how he had touched me, how it made me feel, how he made me feel.

When I was ready, I dressed and drank the cool glass of water Alex had left for me and when I felt composed, I went back to the room where Alex was waiting.

'Thanks Alex, that was just the best massage I have ever had. Really it was.'

'Thank you, Rebecca, that's very kind of you. I hope everything met with your expectations?'

'Oh yes, it most certainly did and more. I think you'll do very well here,'

'I hope so Rebecca, it's a big risk for me coming down to London. I guess I must rely on Oliver to help me get up and running in the short term.'

I couldn't help but wonder why he would get into bed with Oliver, business wise so to speak, they were so different and appeared to have nothing in common. In the normal scheme of things Oliver and Alex would never be friends or associates, but maybe they weren't friends at all. Oliver was only interested in two things, money and himself. I could imagine Oliver was using Alex for his own ends, in some way, and that made me feel suspicious and a little angry. I used my mobile phone to locate an Uber and saw there was one, just two minutes away.

'I've a feeling you don't really need anybody to help you out,' I said, 'You seem more than capable from what I can tell, although of course I could also do with a little more convincing. You haven't forgotten that I have another two sessions promised to me?'

'No, I haven't forgotten. Why don't you take my card and you can ring me on my mobile any time?'

He handed me his card and brushed against his hand as I took it from him. Oh those hands, I wanted more of them.

'Listen, I'd better go there's an Uber on its way.'

'Let me walk you to the door.'

I followed him through to the unfinished reception area and he unlocked the door for me. Stepping out into the street I turned to say goodbye and automatically both of us leaned forward to offer a kiss on the cheek. Wow, that was a surprise to us both I thought and yet it felt so natural and oh my, did he smell so good?

I sat in the back of the car on my way home. I felt relaxed and at peace with the world and I didn't want a pointless conversation with the taxi driver to spoil that. My mobile rang however and a look at the screen told me it was Oliver, my peace was spoiled already. As soon as I answered the call, I knew it was a mistake, it would have been so much easier to just let it ring out and go to voice mail.

'Hi Oliver.'

'Hi Rebecca, Just ringing to see how it went?'

'How what went?'

'Your massage with Alex. Everything okay I hope?'

How did Oliver know I'd chosen today for my appointment with Alex? I don't remember telling him.'

'Oh yes, it was fine thank you.' I replied curiously.

'Great, I knew you'd find him to your liking. I think Alex and I are going to do some good business together. Alex is the sort of guy you can trust don't you think?'

'Well, yes I suppose he is. Listen, Oliver, my battery is going flat and I think we could lose the call at any moment.'

With that I ended the call and turned my phone off so he couldn't ring back. I could see the driver looking at me in the rear-view mirror. I returned his stare with a shrug of the shoulders. 'Flat battery.' I said.

So call it women's intuition, sixth sense or just downright experience of men who were worthless but just lately everything Oliver did made me dislike him even more. If it hadn't been for his big announcement of this latest business venture, I would have ended our relationship in the restaurant that night.

But I was glad I hadn't because I had met Alex. For the life of me, however, I couldn't understand how Alex and Oliver had formed a business relationship. They had nothing in common with each other, Oliver's obsession with money was the only thing that drove him, so what was it that bought the two of them together? To the odd thing about Oliver, even though he had this obsession with money, he never seemed to have any which was hard to understand as he came from a well-to-do family. Foolishly I had loaned him £5,000 for his Hungarian restaurant venture, which I was pretty sure I would never see again. He was just a dreamer, always talking the talk but never actually seeing anything through to fruition. The minute there was an obstacle, or any challenge, he would ditch his latest venture for another. Why couldn't he just stick to his art appraisal work? He knew his stuff and even I had to agree he was an expert in his field, why couldn't he be satisfied with that?

I'd lost count of the unrealised ventures he had dreamed up. Each one would be a winner and he expected me to be supportive of him when all the time he showed little or no interest in how my business was faring. Actually, he showed very little interest in me at all. I had long since given up encouraging him to accompany me when I went shopping for clothes. All he ever did was mope about, dragging his feet and on the last occasion we were out together I caught him ogling at other women trying clothes on. And don't get me started about him leaving the toilet seat up.

My biggest regret most recently however was when I tried to take his mind off the failure of his travel agency by showing him the old drawing I kept in the safe. What was I thinking? Yes, it had cheered him up considerably, but he had become obsessed with it, quizzing me constantly about its history. It had been a family secret for a long time and like an idiot I'd shared it with a man I was beginning to despise. Oliver liked to pretend he was tough and decisive, but actually he was dreamer, wishing his life away. He wanted a magical wishbone, but actually he needed a backbone. And why was I going out with a man who dressed so badly? Wear a suit for business certainly, but did he have to wear one everywhere we went? Where was his sense of style? I'd tried coaching him about clothes but had given up. He was his own man when it came to style, if you could call it style, if you could call him a man? Alex was a man, and I sat back in my seat, closed my eyes and tried to imagine him touching me again. I reached for my neck and realised the tension that was there was all gone. Alex, I'd dream about Alex and yet was that the right thing to do? Perhaps I had been here before.

***

Have you ever tried to do the right thing in the wrong situation? You may as well give up before you begin. I was faced with this dilemma whilst I was studying in Rome. Of course it's no problem at all if you're single, but when you're supposed to have a boyfriend back in London, then what do you do? Well, I have to admit that it was a case of out of sight out of mind I'm sad to say. But what is a young girl supposed to do in my situation, walk around blind folded without looking at any other man?

I've always enjoyed window shopping, you know, checking out the goods on offer without intending to buy. Well, it works for clothes and it certainly works for men too… especially in Rome. That's where a little self-control comes in handy. Just because I see a Gucci handbag I like doesn't mean I can have it, not that it stops a girl dreaming. As a wise woman once told me, *'When on a diet, those with self-control will reach for the apple instead of the cake.'* The thing is… I love cake.

My time studying in Rome presented a real challenge to my powers of restraint. Francesca my Italian friend and fellow student had introduced me to so many of her *amici* and she had a veritable entourage of friends.

Now I don't know if you've ever been to Italy, but if you have, you may have noticed groups of girls and boys going around, socialising together. It's the way things are over there and I'm not sure if it's the culture or the good weather, either way it's nice to see.

You might see them outside a Gelateria or sharing pizza together and they are never any bother to anyone, they're just out having fun. Back home in London I used to go around with my girlfriends and that carried on when I passed my teenage years and it became nights on the town with the girls.

As they say, 'when in Rome,' so far be it for me to go against tradition and that is where I met Fabio.

What can I say about Fabio? He was beautiful. I know, saying a man is beautiful seems odd, but he was. Tall, strong jawline, sultry dark eyes and such lovely hair, the man was an Adonis. I was hoping it was only me that was stuck by his beauty but as I studied the reaction of the other girls in the group, I could see that I was not alone in being attracted to him and I was suddenly jealous. Why, I asked myself, am I feeling jealous about a man I have only just met for the first time. He might already have a girlfriend. It seemed logical that such a hunk of a man would, but even so I just couldn't help myself. 'Stop it,' my conscience said, 'you have a boyfriend back in London'… and then he spoke to me.

'When you going to come for a drink with me?' He asked.

I was taken aback and so was my conscience, which was also struck dumb. I realised that he had asked me in English, maybe so that his other admirers couldn't understand what he was saying.

'I don't think I can do that. I have a boyfriend back in London.' What the hell was I saying?

Fortunately, my answer made no difference to Fabio's interest in me. 'It is only a drink,' he reasoned. 'But maybe you English girls love the attention and like to play hard to get, no?'

He was right, I loved the attention and I would play hard to get. 'No thank you Fabio, I have far too much studying to do.'

The look on his face told me he liked a challenge.

I had agreed to a trip out with my university friends to the Villa Borghese Gardens, which are 16th Century Gardens combining art and nature in central Rome. It's sort of a Roman equivalent to London's Regent's Park with the Museum District set inside of it. I was keen to visit the art museums amidst the beautiful landscape and a group of us had agreed to take a picnic. But who should show up uninvited? It was the beautiful Fabio of course.

Our little group thought nothing of it when he explained that by pure coincidence he was taking a leisurely stroll through the park when he came upon us. But I think both of us knew the real reason he had shown up.

Fabio was very knowledgeable about the history of the park as we walked side by side through the gardens. He also knew much about the art on display in the museum, which naturally meant we had something in common to talk about. My defences, or what little I was pretending to myself I had, were soon torn down, and we spent a wonderful afternoon together.

Playing hard to get is not a strength I possess because by the end of our visit I had agreed to go out for pizza with him the following evening. Now please don't chastise me for being weak, but there was something about Fabio that made all women he came into contact with go weak at the knees. So why should I be the exception?

The Roman weather makes it easy to decide what to wear. I had bought a classic red crepe-de-sheen, mid-length, off the shoulder Bardot dress from a small Italian boutique in Rome the previous summer. Having a local friend like Francesca paid dividends as she gave me the names of all the local, independent clothes stores that suited my student pocket.

I knew this little number might raise some eyebrows, not merely because of the colour and style, but that it held my waist in so I looked thin around the midriff and showed off the tan I'd preserved whilst in Italy. What to do with my long hair, however, presented a challenge. Three hours later I settled on the very first hairstyle I trialled to begin with after experimenting with half a dozen. It was a simple style, my hair swept into a one sided pony tail, falling loosely onto my shoulder.

Maybe I should just ring Fabio and cancel the date night altogether? That would be pointless as he'd just keep bothering me all over again, my confused conscience told me, until I eventually caved in.

No, I'd go just this once and that would be it. He probably has a whole bunch of annoying habits that would put me off for life anyway, I told myself.

All my fears and anxiety cleared once I met with Fabio. He was so attentive and humorous, which is very rare given English isn't his native language. He greeted me with a rose, which was a lovely surprise and like a true gentleman he opened the door leading me to our reserved spot, pulling a chair out from under the table to allow me to sit first.

The magnificent aroma wafting from the ovens in the kitchen and as I looked at the menu, I could see that choosing a pizza would not be easy, especially with the butterflies doing their little dance in my stomach.

Fabio recommended the chef's special, but I went with a plain and simple one.

'You look so beautiful tonight *cara*,' Fabio told me. 'You are very Italian.'

I blushed and thought the same of him given his beautiful attire, beautiful hair and beautiful face.

He reached for my hand and I didn't pull away, even when the pizza's arrived. Eating was mechanical and my taste buds had gone on strike. Fabio leant across the table to gently wipe a spot of stray sauce from the corner of my mouth with the napkin. That was embarrassing.

My nerves had rendered my stomach with so many butterflies that I only managed one or two mouthfuls, so I decided to take my Pizza to go to, but only if I ever wanted to eat again of course.

Weight control has been an issue for most of my life. When I was very young, I contracted pneumonia and spent a long time in hospital recovering. I lost 50lb of my little body as a result, which was quite a lot considering how young I was. When I had recovered and was discharged, my mother fed me all the foods I loved and craved; any food, any time, night or day. Naturally as a result I put all the weight I'd lost back on again and lots more besides. Now, I was never a skinny child by any means but having being bullied at junior school and then as a teenager at high school, where competitiveness about appearance was rife, I failed to escape the taunts about my Yo-Yo weight. The trouble is that becoming upset only leads to self-medicating on food so that the vicious cycle continues until I received a massive wake-up call when someone mistook me for my mother's sister.

I joined Weight-Watchers and for the second time in my life I lost 50lbs. Only this time the weight loss suited me. This was an ultimate game changer as not only had I reached a milestone, that some said I would never achieve, but I looked and felt completely different.

So there I was, picking at my food with the beautiful Fabio. I sipped at my wine, relaxed in his company whilst he drank Peroni, finished his meal with an espresso, followed by an Amaro.

He looked very relaxed, very self-assured, leaning back with one arm draped over the back of his chair as he gazed at me from across the table. 'Let us go back to my apartment now *cara* and get to know each other better,' he said

'Wait a minute where did that come from,' I thought. So I asked him. 'Wait a minute Fabio, where did that come from.'

He looked confused. Maybe it was the English phrase, *where did that come from.* Perhaps that didn't translate very well into Italian.

'Oh Rebecca,' he said. 'I like you and you like me so we go back to my apartment and we make love. That is what you English girls like also, no?'

'Oh, so all of a sudden I'm not all that Italian? When it suits you, I'm English. Well no, not this English girl,' I snapped back at him. Picked up my handbag, grabbed my pizza box and stormed out of the restaurant.

Back at my own tiny apartment I couldn't believe that Fabio only had eyes for me because he thought I was an easy lay, and I wasn't. Why had I fallen for him so easily?

I held the last slice of pizza between my fingers and told myself I was better than that; I had a boyfriend in London and I was doing the right thing.

'Boy, this pizza is good,' I said out loud, swallowing the last mouthful.

53

CHAPTER 4

I'd been finding difficulty to concentrate at work in the days since my encounter with Alex for two reasons. Firstly, I couldn't stop daydreaming about the way he had touched me and how he had made me feel. Lucy kept asking me if I was okay because she was concerned about me staring into space all the time. But the other thing was the questionable working relationship between Alex and Oliver. I don't know why it bothered me but it did. Was it because Oliver's ideas were usually weird, out there concepts and this was one that made sense? Or was it because his motivation was to acquire lots of money in the shortest time possible, so here he was, partnering with someone skilled. Maybe Oliver was looking at a long-term relationship this time? Yet it made no sense and troubled me.

I also wondered why and how Alex had agreed to accept Oliver's offer to provide him with the set-up costs. If it was money he needed then maybe I could help him out? Maybe I could and I wouldn't be interested in skimming any profits. I would be more than happy to offer Alex an interest free loan. I was sure he would pay me back when he'd built up his customer base. I'd decided I would offer to buy Oliver out; after all, he owed me a considerable amount of money that I doubted I would ever see again. I would become Alex's new sleeping partner.

Oliver had been out of the town for a few days on a business trip, but I'd left him a message to call by the gallery on his return because this was something I wanted to discuss with him. We arranged to meet on Thursday afternoon, Lucy's day off, so we could have our discussion in private. My message asked him to call in at around an hour before the gallery closing time. It was a decision that I would soon regret.

The gallery was empty at 4.30pm when Oliver opened the door. He was about to step inside when a short, stocky man barged past him and immediately a cold swell of fear washed through my body.

'Hello Rebecca, how lovely to see you again,' the man said, smiling an icy smile.

'Mr Robins,' was all I could reply.

'It's been far too long since I visited your father's gallery. Oh, sorry Rebecca. It's your gallery now, isn't it? I was very sad to hear of your father's passing. He and I went back a long way.'

Micky Robins had been a sort of acquaintance of my father, but I could never figure out why. It was true that Robins had bought a few pieces of high value art from the gallery back then and that all seemed legitimate. Even so, I recalled his visits to the gallery and how there was always a tense feeling when Robins was in the room. Perhaps the tension could be explained by the rumours suggesting he was possibly one of London East End's most notorious crooks. That tension returned now. Robins took a seat opposite me at my desk.

'So I was thinking it was about time I invested in some art once again,' he announced.

'Art can be a very good investment,' I replied shakily. 'But I'm not sure I have anything in our inventory that would interest you.'

'Maybe you have or maybe you haven't because today I'm interested in something quite special, quite unique, something that was thought lost.' Robins said.'

'Well, if it's lost, I'm sure I won't be able to find it for you. I'm an art dealer, not a magician.'

Robins laughed, unruffled by my abrupt reply. 'Ah but your grandfather was a magician wasn't he Rebecca? He could make things disappear in a blink of an eye.'

I remained silent and stony faced as Robins smiled and continued his story.

'Like when your dear Grandpa was working for the Monument's Men at the end of World War Two. Combing through Italy, tracking down and recovering priceless works of art that the Nazis were trying to carry back to the Fatherland. Then would you believe it, he discovered something so rare and so precious that he couldn't possibly give it up. So he kept it for himself.'

'That's ridiculous' I snapped.

'I agree it sounds ridiculous that Grandpa could have discovered a genuine Michelangelo, but after all that was his job wasn't it? Perhaps it's also ridiculous that your Poppa kept it a secret ever since. Keeping Michelangelo's Leda and the Swan a secret from the world.'

My face blanched. 'Are you seriously suggesting that my Grandfather miraculously discovered a priceless work of art, long considered lost? Somehow secretly kept it for himself with nobody knowing? He would have wanted such a find to be shown to the world, why the fame of discovering it would have been reward itself.'

'Yes, that's right, it would. But what if he found some original sketches? Work Michelangelo would have done in preparation to create a masterpiece? It might not have been obvious in the beginning but after a while, when he'd had time to study it and its true identity was realised, just to own such a thing, to be able to look at it and know it's yours, that would be enough for any man who appreciates things of such beauty.'

There was silence in the room, Robins and I stared each other out across the desk, locking eyes to see who would break first. Oliver remained frozen to the spot, as still as a statue, rigid with fear. He held his breath as Robins slowly reached inside his jacket and equally slowly withdrew a rectangular slip of paper.

'Here is a cheque for a £100,000 Rebecca, that's a lot of money for you to enjoy. I give you this cheque, you give me the drawing.' Robins held the piece of paper high for me to see.

'There is no such drawing, no such sketch,' I calmly but firmly explained. 'I wish there was, but there isn't. I don't know where you heard such an outrageous story so I suggest you save your money because I can't help you and now I'd like you to leave, please.'

Again there was a long silence as Robins carefully folded the check in half and returned it to his jacket pocket. He rose from his chair smiling, keeping eye contact with me. He shrugged his shoulders, turned and walked toward the door without saying a word. As Robins reached the door, he stopped and directed his menacing stare at Oliver who, almost immediately felt the colour drain from his face in fear. Quickly, timidly, Oliver opened the door for Robins to leave. Oliver had been holding his breath, for how long he couldn't remember, but he let it all out now that Robins had left.

'My God, Rebecca,' Oliver said breathlessly. 'How would he know about the drawing?'

'I don't know,' I replied exuding an air of calm even though inside my heart was pounding. 'Robins and my father had a strange relationship back in the day. Maybe Poppa said something, I don't know'

'I can't think why Robins and your Father would ever be friends,' suggested Oliver. 'And a hundred thousand pounds for it? That drawing is worth one hundred times that.'

'I wish the damn thing never existed,' I confessed. 'And to be honest, I really don't know what the bloody thing is anyway. Is it just a sketch on an old piece of paper or is it really something more? God, I wish it had disappeared along with the finished painting'

'Oh no,' disagreed Oliver 'It would be a real pity if that disappeared too. It's too beautiful.'

I stared at Oliver, many thoughts going through my head. He had been no help during the confrontation with Robins, how I wished I had never confided in Oliver and revealed the sketch to him. It felt like a millstone around my neck, but even now, after the sense of danger that had just filled the gallery, all Oliver could think of was that wretched drawing and its value. Why had Nonno kept it when he should have revealed it, given it to the world to enjoy if it was genuine? Far from being priceless, it was a liability. And there was Oliver grinning at me like nothing had happened. He was useless, and right at that moment I knew I hated him. Oliver was not the one; I knew that for certain now. I had just dealt with Robins on my own and I knew now that I didn't need Oliver. I didn't need him now and I wouldn't need him later. I needed Alex and right at that moment I wanted him desperately.

CHAPTER 5

Using his office phone number I left a voicemail asking Alex to meet me at the Cuore Rosso restaurant, I needed to be amongst familiar people in a familiar place and the events of the previous day had unsettled me.

Lucy was back in the gallery as it was Friday so I wasn't alone, but I had felt nervous about being there and a repeat performance with Robins occurring.

Even though it was a Friday evening and all the best restaurants would be fully booked, I knew Luigi would find me a table and sure enough he obliged, finding me a quiet spot out of sight at the back of the restaurant. I arrived early and had already asked for a bottle of wine before Alex joined me.

Maybe I was drinking too much, I was already halfway through the bottle but I felt I needed something to steady my nerves. What was I doing? Here I was waiting for a man I hardly knew for a reason I couldn't really understand. This seemed very familiar however. I thought about my time in Rome and another man in another restaurant. If I was being honest with myself, I knew why I was there.

Just the day before something frightening had burst into my world and scared me. Yes, I had to admit it; Robins had scared me a lot. But the thing that terrified me was how did he know about the drawing? I had told nobody, other than

Oliver of course, and I made him swear to me he hadn't told a soul.

The look of terror on Oliver's face during Robins' visit suggested that Oliver couldn't possibly know a man like that. Why would he?

Even so, Robins appeared to know bits and pieces of a story that even I wasn't totally sure of. Frighteningly he knew I possessed a piece of artwork and I was pretty sure he would not give up easily. Yet what was I going to tell Alex? I couldn't tell him everything. Already it appeared too many people knew about the ancient sketch, if it was ancient and genuine.

Whatever I would tell Alex I needed to decide right now as here he was making his way through the tables towards me.

'Hello,' he said.

Just one word… *hello* and I felt better already.

'How are you? It's good to see you again Rebecca, you sounded a little agitated on the phone so I wondered what was up. Are you okay?'

I wasn't okay when I had phoned Alex. I'd made a knee-jerk reaction following the scare that Robins had given me and Oliver was no help. I needed help.

'Err well, I'd had some things on my mind, you know, but I thought it would be nice to see you again.' I said. Which was all I could think of to say, although it was perfectly true?

'Okay,' he replied unconvinced, 'but you said we had something important to discuss.'

Yes, I remembered saying that now. Robins had scared me and that was why I had contacted Alex. But that little voice inside told me to hold my tongue until I had thought this out properly. Then quick as a flash my brain engaged and reminded me about my idea of buying Oliver out to become Alex's business partner.

My mind was a jumble of mixed emotions, unwelcome feelings and difficult decisions.

For example, what I should wear for this evening was a real ordeal. Experience had taught me how to dress for business, fitness or just casual wear. This was entirely different because I was dressing for Alex and naturally I wanted to make a good impression. It was just a business meeting after all, I told myself. Not that I believed it. And so I did what I usually do under the circumstances and conducted my own private fashion show back in the bedroom at home. You know the one where you try on a dozen outfits and go with the first one you tried on to begin with.

Even knowing the discomfort it would give me, I chose a demure jade green dress with flattering *to die for,* figure hugging style. Uncomfortable because it was a fitted garment, round necked with nipped waist and bodice. (I have a thing about my waist as you may have noticed?) The dress had long sleeves with a flattering fish tail effect to just above the knee to compliment my hips. (I have a thing about my hips too).

This outfit fitted me like a second skin with very little room to breathe, or eat for that matter. It made me feel a little better about myself as it pushed everything back into the places they were supposed to be in. The dress gave the impression of an hourglass figure where not all the sand had run to the bottom. I wore it alongside black opaque thigh-highs with fresh lace edging and black suede leather stilettoes which had a sexy bow detail on the back of the heel. Shoes after all are the most important accessory to the dress. Maybe they are the most important?

Was it all too risqué, this attention to detail? Although I had only met him a couple of times I was drawn to Alex and perhaps subconsciously I was dealing with this as a first date?

And it gets even better. Under this outfit I wore my sensually alluring, *take me to bed* lingerie. A black vintage plunge longline bra and thong set; designed to extenuate my figure, inspiring oodles of confidence. Irresistible, a combination of sheer mesh, soft lace and an audacious, asset emphasising plunge. As any good woman will tell you, well fitted, and in this case French, chic lingerie is an essential wardrobe must have to go under any fitted garment. So many women get this wrong and I would not be one of them. A lot of effort I know, but Alex was worth it I told myself.

When Alex first caught sight of me, I could see from his diluted pupils all my dressing efforts had paid off.

'Rebecca, wow, you look beautiful.' Alex said.

'You don't look so bad yourself.' I replied

And sure enough he looked and smelled fabulous. I couldn't be certain but his navy single breasted blazer looked designer brand. Maybe Paul Smith, Armani or Hugo Boss. Together with light blue Chinos and matching shirt with cut away collar with sleeves displaying sterling silver cufflinks. This was a match made in heaven, a celestial gift indeed, a man who knows how to take care of himself was a rare thing and I had to muster all my resolve to stop myself being distracted by this handsomely alluring man despite the circumstance under which we were meeting. Maybe the wine was helping?

'Thank you for meeting me at short notice Alex, I really appreciate you giving your time. Now let's get down to business shall we?' What was I saying… let's get down to business… really?

'No problem whatsoever,' replied Alex 'I did say you should feel free to contact me again if ever you needed to. What can I do for you?'

'What can't you do, I thought wickedly?' I reluctantly withdrew my gaze away from Alex to stare at my business file on the table to regain my thoughts. Yes, it was definitely the wine.

'I'll just come straight to the point, after giving some considerable thought I'd like to make you a business proposal. I'd like to ask Oliver if I can buy him out and that I become your business partner.'

'Err, I'm flattered Rebecca and thank you for your vote of confidence. Does Oliver know about this?' Alex asked, phased.

'No, but he will do shortly, I wanted to run it with you first.' I replied.

'For my part, it's really very generous of you but not necessary at this stage. Besides, I have an agreement with Oliver. I trust in his business sense completely.'

'That's just it Alex, I'm not convinced he's the right partner or has any relevant experience to offer you given his previous background. Surely the main aim is for your business to become financially successful. This means incorporating a partner who will add value by contributing some business acumen to compliment your excellent professional skill-set, which I believe I'm better qualified to offer.'

'That's very astute of you Rebecca but there's no need really, I'm both touched and flattered you would consider this. I have a partner in Oliver and there's really no going back now, I'm a man of my word and I'm tied to him at the moment anyway.'

My ego dented, not thrown by his rejection but thrown by this comment of being tied to Oliver. What did he mean by that?

'I see, don't you at least want to think about it?' I said almost pleadingly. I was certain he was making a big mistake given he didn't know Oliver as I did.

'Nope, like I said, I'm in safe hands.' Alex reassured me.

'That's debatable.' I remarked.

Alex could see his refusal had offended me.

'Let me order you another drink, what can I get you?' He offered.

'A gin and tonic please.' I asked abruptly, 'Make it a double.'

'I haven't offended you have I Rebecca?'

'Offend me, don't be silly.' I assured Alex.

'Good, as that's the last thing I want to do, to you of all people. I hope we can remain friends, we can can't we?' Alex asked cautiously.

'Sure,' I replied in my best convincing voice.

'Let me buy you dinner to show there's no hard feeling?'

'That won't be necessary, I won't be staying, I have work to do.' I said lying through my teeth.

'Now I know I've upset you. In fact I would go as far to say that you appear quite stressed,' he said.

Had he really noticed that I was indeed stressed out? Was it that obvious to him?

'I tell you what.' He continued. 'Why don't you drop by my office and we could try out some stress relieving hypnotherapy?'

Suddenly the thought of getting up and leaving was forgotten. Alex was offering to show more of his skills to me and was I really going to spoil it all by getting upset? 'Oh, I'm not sure about that Alex. I do like a massage but I've never even considered hypnotherapy,' I said.

'You should try it. The human mind is a wonderful thing and with the right suggestions hypnotherapy can help in many ways. Why don't you try it? Look, I'm sorry if I have upset you and to make it up you can have a calming massage first followed by a little hypnosis. I promise you'll feel much better.'

The thought of Alex touching me again, plus the effects of half a bottle of wine and a large G&T softened my resolve. 'Well okay, but as long as I don't go around barking like a dog afterwards,' I replied, smiling at him again now.

'That's not what hypnotherapy is all about,' Alex replied seriously. 'Stage hypnotists give us professional therapists a bad name. At the end of the day Rebecca, it's about trust between the therapist and the client?

'Let's give it a go then.'

'Okay, great that's settled then and anyway, you have a gift certificate to use up.'

My offer of a partnership foiled, I needed to show a deeper level of trust than before. If I refused his treatment now, then Alex wouldn't trust me and how genuine my offer was.

We both laughed at that and relaxed in each other's company.

'I'm starving,' remarked Alex. 'Why do we order a bite to eat after which we can go straight to my office? Trust me Rebecca, once you've experienced this you will feel amazing.'

'Absolutely,' I agreed. 'I seem to have an appetite suddenly. Luigi, il menu per favore.'

***

The eagerness inside me, the anticipation of Alex's wonderful hands touching my body again was sky high. Gone were the nerves of our previous encounter replaced by the expectation that something wonderfully sensual was about to happen again.

As before, Alex left the treatment room to allow me to prepare myself. This time I remembered not to throw my bra across the room, carefully placing my garments on the chair.

The wine and the food at Luigi's restaurant were having a soporific effect on my mind and body. Unlike the last time that I lay here, I was not nervous or tense. Instead, I was already calm as I lay on the massage table, awaiting my skilful, handsome masseuse.

Alex had already briefed me about what to expect from hypnosis. I was sceptical at first, but his eloquent and knowledgeable description had put my mind at ease. I would not be under some sort of mystical influence where I would lose control, he explained, but rather my mind would enter a different, heightened state of consciousness. I would feel calm and relaxed where my subconscious would be open to new ideas and suggestions. Alex reassured me that during the process it wouldn't be a case of being under his command. If I didn't want to follow the suggestions he gave me, then my mind wouldn't accept them and more importantly, only a willing individual could be hypnotised. If they didn't want to be hypnotised, then they couldn't be.

There was a gentle knock at the door and I gave Alex permission to enter.

No words were spoken between us as he quietly walked about the room to turn on the gentle music, to arrange the sheet about my body and to prepare his hands with the massage oil.

I could hear the sound of liquid being applied to his hands, and I eagerly awaited the feel of his warm touch to my skin. Then when it happened I let out a soft involuntary moan as long, slow, rhythmic strokes eased up and down my sides and back, up to my shoulders and down my arms.

This wasn't the same as my first time with Alex. The massage wasn't applied with the same firm pressure as before; the pressure designed to ease the tension in my neck and the knot in my shoulders, but neither was his touch light nor soft. Somehow there was a new intensity to the way his hands moved over my body. It was sensual, it was erotic, it was carnal.

Alex's skill gave away my heightened senses and excitement. He knew his responsibility at that moment was to calm me to the point of drowsiness. Slowly but surely I began to relax and yield to the touch of his velvet hands. I was in heaven, and just when I thought my feelings of bliss couldn't get any better, Alex began to talk gently to me.

His voice was calm and deep, his words soothing and persuasive. His hands had soothed

70

my body and now his soft tones were quietening my mind.

Alex asked me to think of my favourite place in nature, somewhere familiar to me where I could be alone. So my mind's eye settled on the rolling Tuscan hills, a place I had spent so many happy family holidays. He encouraged me to think of a clear blue sky and a warm, beautiful day and imagine how the sun played on my body. I began to imagine how the sun made each part of my body feel.

Could I recall every word he said to me? No, I am not sure I could recall that every little detail that Alex described was becoming believable and real to me.

I remember the day becoming night. I remember the feeling of weightlessness as I floated up into a perfectly clear night sky. I remember counting the bright stars in the sky.

The feeling of weightless euphoria was pleasing and I was now suspended in a deep, deep trance and magically transported to a beautiful garden that Alex had imprinted in my inner mind.

The thing I do remember about the tranquil garden I was in was how I could actually feel the soft blades of grass on the souls of my feet as I walked barefoot in between beautiful flowers and trees. The sound of the wind rustling the leaves and the buzz of insects were as real to me as anything I had ever encountered in my conscious state.

In my deepening state of sub-consciousness I was soon at a gate which led to a beach. Everything described there to me was so real and pleasing that I was eager and willing to be drawn in to dream. Somehow the desire to open the gate and step onto the warm soft sand of the beach was too compelling to resist. I knew that Alex would be waiting for me there.

I could see him, waiting for me by the water's edge. I walked towards him and with each step I took my feelings of happiness increased and so did my feelings of trust and being safe when near Alex. My subconscious mind accepting everything I desired.

We walked hand in hand along the shore, warm water gently lapping at our feet. There was no one else on the beach, we were completely alone and I felt protected. We came upon a deckchair which I sat on. It was the most comfortable chair that I had ever experienced, despite deckchairs being notoriously uncomfortable. Closing my eyes on the perfect day, I could feel the warm sun on my face and hear gentle waves lapping on the sand.

Slowly and calmly, I came back to consciousness in the dimly lit treatment room. I felt incredibly relaxed and content, in a state of tranquil peace. Lifting my head from the table, I looked around and was disappointed to see that Alex wasn't there in the room.

Swinging my legs around to sit on the edge of the table, I noticed my clothes had been folded neatly and placed on the chair, in stark contrast to how I'd left them in a hurry to undress.

On top of the pile was a small, rectangular card and hopping to the floor I picked up the card. It was Alex's business card, complete with address and his private mobile number. Smiling to myself, I held it to my chest. It was clear what Alex was saying to me now. I quickly grabbed my clothes dressed quickly.

I looked at Alex's card and understood most clearly and definitely that I didn't need Oliver the boy child anymore. I needed Alex.

CHAPTER 6

Once again concentrating on work had been difficult for me following the hypnosis I had enjoyed with Alex. There was a strange yearning inside of me that was difficult to describe. I knew I wanted to be with Alex again. I wanted to feel his hands on my body again. I wanted to feel his touch and to hear his persuasive voice in my mind. Although I knew everything I had felt during the hypnotic spell were not real, to me it was as tangible as anything I'd ever experienced and I wanted more. But this time it had to be physical, actual and absolutely for real.

Oliver hadn't been in contact since that last meeting, which was a relief. I had no desire to see the grinning little fool again. What did I ever see in him?

Visits to my mother at the nursing home however had kept me grounded. Mum was having a good period where some of those memories that seemed to have been lost forever, reappeared again, albeit briefly. We talked about some of the small pieces of art I had installed in my mother's room and this helped re-kindle happy memories of when and where Poppa had discovered each work of art and how beautiful they were. It was strange how such a debilitating illness could not erase those early times from my mother's mind, which was a blessing amidst her curse. But for me, the only thing I could recall were visions of Alex.

I had looked at Alex's card repeatedly, often gently touching it with my fingers so softly as if it were an actual part of him. I had been putting it off for days now, but I would phone him. It was strange for me to be so nervous, that wasn't like me at all. When I got home that evening, from a day at the gallery and a visit to Mum, I sat at my dining table, Alex's card in one hand and my phone in the other. I would call, I would do it now.

With my thumb I selected each number in turn, and poised over the call button. I chickened out and deleted each number one by one.

Instead, I took the easy way out and sent him a text.

Alex, why don't you come and visit at my gallery

43 North Ave

Love Rebecca xxx

Two minutes later my cell chirped a reply.

'*I'd love to, see you tomorrow gorgeous xxx,*'

Thursday was a good day for Alex to be visiting the gallery. There would be just the two of us in the gallery so no-one would see our meeting, no-one to ask any awkward questions.

Once again deciding what to wear had been a difficult decision for me. Should I be businesslike as usual or maybe dress a little more sexily? What if customers come into the gallery, how would they react to what I was wearing? I even started to worry about my choice of underwear so much so, that I could not decide whether I should wear regular or best underwear, if there was such a thing? I decided on a visit to Victoria's

75

Secret to purchase a new set altogether. I would normally treat myself to new underwear when I was visiting Italy, but maybe it was time for something a little different?

Quite what I expected to be doing to reveal new panties and bra in the gallery I wasn't sure, but it felt like the sort of occasion that called for new underwear.

But the dilemma wasn't helped whilst browsing through the new collections. Everything I looked at seemed like it would be more suited to a burlesque show than a successful, sexy business woman. In the end I played it safe and went for a simple matching set in black silk satin, edged with black lace. At least the balcony bra I selected would push my assets to the fore and give a hint of what was beneath the figure hugging black dress I would wear.

Shoes were another issue and as I unlocked the door to the gallery, I wished that I had chosen shorter heels. The five inch, pencil thin heels I wore that morning had already proved an issue walking to and from the underground.

Alex hadn't said what time he would call at the gallery, I hoped it would be early in the day because concentrating on my work would prove difficult. I spent the first hour of the morning moving the stapler, hole-punch and phone around the desk to find the perfect position and then moving them all over again. I even moved the position of the desk so that when Alex entered through the door, he would get a perfect view of me.

I wasn't looking at the front door when I heard it open, I was repositioning the desk tidy again and the smile on my face as I looked up in anticipation was quickly replaced by an open-mouthed stare. Walking into the gallery was Robins, and he wasn't alone. He was followed through the door by a thickset, overweight man in an ill-fitting suit carrying a black briefcase.

'Good morning Rebecca,' Robins greeted me with false politeness, and sitting down without waiting for an invitation to do so.

I shifted uncomfortably in my seat but straightened myself to defy my visitors. 'What do you want Mr. Robins? I told you the last time you were here that I had nothing that would interest you. Now I'd like you gentlemen to leave please.'

'Oh come now Rebecca, don't be so unfriendly. I might have something that could be of interest to you.'

'That I very much doubt,' I replied.

Robins nodded to the thickset man who stepped forward and placed the briefcase on the desk in front of me.

'What's that for?' I asked.

'Open it. I think you'll like what's inside.'

Very carefully I drew the case towards me and unlocked the two brass catches with the thumb of each hand. The catches sprang open and I lifted the lid. Inside were neat stacks of cash, arranged in rows with their paper bands showing that each stack was worth £1,000.

'Maybe offering you a cheque was a mistake on my part,' explained Robins 'I'm sure that cash is much more appropriate in this case and just to show how sincere my offer is, I've made it up to a nice round quarter of a million.'

'I already told you, there is nothing here for you,' I replied firmly, closing the case again. I clicked the locks shut and turned the case around so that the handle faced Robins.

'Please take your money and go,' I insisted.

'Don't be so hasty now. You can do a lot with that money and what's more the Inland Revenue would never know. It's just a private business deal between friends.'

'You're not my friend Mr. Robins and I'm not asking again. Please leave.'

Robins folded his arms. He clearly wasn't planning on going anywhere and the false smile he wore was also gone, replaced by an angry expression and with narrowing eyes.

'I've been quite generous to you Rebecca, but you're trying my patience. We both know you have a Michelangelo original sketch for the lost painting of Leda and the Swan hidden away somewhere. I'm pretty sure your grandfather found it and kept it for himself when he should have surrendered it to the authorities and all the while it's hidden from view so that nobody can enjoy it. What's the point in holding onto it if you can't enjoy it? Now I, on the other hand, would enjoy owning it immensely and I'm sure you would enjoy this money.'

He turned the case back round to me so the handle was facing me again. I stood up sharply and being as brave as I could, shouted, 'Get out and get out now before I call the police, I'm not asking again.' My hand moved toward the phone.

The thickset man moved a step closer toward me. Robins raised his hand and the man stopped.

'And tell them what Rebecca? That I'm trying to buy stolen goods from you?'

'I don't have any stolen goods,' I snapped in reply, but I couldn't see his next move and I was frightened now.

Just in time the door to the gallery opened and Alex entered. He took stock of the situation quickly and could easily tell something was very wrong.

'Is there a problem here Rebecca?' He asked, knowing that there was.

'I'd like these gentlemen to leave my gallery.' I managed to answer, my heart pounding in my chest.

'Gentlemen, I believe the lady would like you to leave now,' Alex explained to the men.

The thickset man moved toward Alex, but he was too heavy and slow to pose a threat to the fit and agile younger man. Alex saw the punch coming way before it reached him, giving him time to easily lean out of the way and allow his attacker's momentum to swing past him, enabling Alex to turn the man and deliver an expertly aimed hard, sharp blow to his kidney. The thickset man crumpled to the floor with a yell of agony. Alex turned his attention to the other unwelcome guest.

Robins raised himself from the chair, trying to retain some dignity. I already had the briefcase held out toward him. Taking the case from my hands, Robins turned to leave, slowly and carefully, unsure of what Alex might do. Without saying a word Robins walked towards the door, ignoring the groans of the thickset man who was trying to raise himself from the floor with no dignity whatsoever. Robins didn't look back, or speak, as he left. His henchman hobbled after him, rubbing his side. Alex closed the door behind him and turned to me to ask.

'What's going on, what did those guys want?'

It was too much for me to answer and I burst into tears, ashamed I had let them get the better of me. Alex walked briskly to me and held me tight in his arms. I placed my moist cheek on his chest and I felt safe again.

'Hey, everything's okay now, they've gone.' Alex reassured me.

I looked up at him, relieved he had arrived just in-time and that he had saved me from danger. Here was a man who could be trusted, exactly as I had felt during my recent hypnotic trance state. I placed my hands up around Alex's neck and pulled his face to meet mine. Our lips touched gently, soft and tender.

'I want you,' I breathed.

'Not here,' he answered. 'Not like this. You're in no state to be at your best. You need to calm down first. I'll drive you back to your place. Come on, lock up here you've done enough for today.'

The drive to my apartment was conducted mostly in silence except for the occasional prompt to tell Alex which route to take. My heart, although steadier now, was still beating strong within my chest so I could almost hear the rhythm. Adrenaline pursed through my system now, not from fear but from excitement. Was I really heading home with Alex? In my mind this was something I had fantasised over so many times. Now from the edge of danger, was my dream about to come true?

I fumbled entering the key in the lock when we arrived at the door of my apartment, Alex's hand covered mine to steady me, helping me guide the key in and open the door.

Once inside the apartment it was Alex who spoke first much to my relief.

'You need a drink, do you have Brandy?' He asked.

'Yes, in a cabinet above the countertops in the kitchen, it's the third one on the left' I said.

'Okay, I'll find it.'

Alex went into the kitchen, following the direction I was pointing to. I stood there waiting, not sure what to do in my own living room. Why was I so nervous? This is what I wanted, wasn't it? Me alone with this gorgeous man at last. I could hear Alex opening and closing cabinet doors.

'Glasses, where do you keep them?' Alex shouted from the kitchen.

'Just along on the right,' I shouted back.

'Okay, found them,' came the reply after more opening and closing of doors.

I hadn't moved and was still standing where Alex had left me when he eventually reappeared with two glasses of brandy, one of which he handed to me. I took the balloon glass from him with both hands, allowing my fingers to brush gently against his as I did so. Alex smiled at me and swirled the glass that was cupped in his other hand, warming the golden liquid.

'So do I need to know what was going on with those two guys?' Alex asked, 'They didn't look like they were art lovers.' He raised the glass to his lips and took a sip.

'Oh them, just a misunderstanding' I replied unconvincingly.

'Hmm, some misunderstanding. It looked like I came along just at the right time?'

'Yes, you did…. thank you Alex.'

He downed the rest of his glass whilst I sipped at mine, still cradling my glass with both hands. Our eyes suddenly locked together, I stared into his over the top of the glass, my lips tasting the warm fluid within.

Then Alex reached across and gently took the glass from my hands and set it on the table beside us. Placing his hands on my shoulders he drew me towards him, bending down slowly to offer his lips up to mine. It was a gentle kiss, gentler than I'd expected, tender but urgent he then held back as if to see what I'd do.

Our faces were so close together. I looked into his eyes and we both held our breath for a moment as if neither of us dared make the next move. I licked my lips hardly believing this man had kissed me and I reciprocated his offer with my lips to his. Once more our kiss was slow and tender. His lips were warm and soft. I could taste the brandy on his warm and delicious mouth. This kiss lasted longer until eventually we pulled away from each other again.

We kissed for a third time, this time deeper, passionately. I cupped his strong masculine jawline in the palms of my hands, his skin was soft to my touch.

Alex's hands began to explore my body, one hand resting between my shoulder blades whilst his other arm encircled my waist. I moved my hands to the back of his head, running my fingers into his luscious thick hair.

He released both hands and placed them on my bottom now, pulling me towards him and I could feel that Alex was already aroused.

'I know you want me,' he affirmed. 'You do want me don't you?'

'Yes,' I whispered.

'Do you trust me?'

Could he tell that my nervousness had rendered me tense, leaving my body taut and rigid. 'Yes, I trust you.' I whispered.

'I've wanted to hold your beautiful body for such a long time,' he breathed in my ear.

He was holding me tight in his arms and I could feel his body against mine. I responded by allowing my hands to explore his neck, his broad shoulders and firm chest. As I kissed his neck I inhaled his aftershave, heightening my senses even more and I swallowed as my mouth moistened and opened.

His mouth pressed harder against mine now as I let myself go completely, our bodies moulding against each other. The man I'd thought of, dreamt of, was now encased in my arms, with his wrapped around mine.

Was this real or was I dreaming again? How could this man know my thoughts, my desires? He knew what I wanted without me needing to tell him.

He lifted me up into his arms and asked, 'Where to?'

I pointed limply to the bedroom door, my laboured breath not allowing me to speak.

He carried me inside and then kicked the door shut behind him.

We made love as the late afternoon sun cast long shadows across our naked bodies. It was dark when he left me, even though I yearned for him to stay. I closed my eyes and smiled to myself. Had I found *the one* this time?

***

Sitting in his own apartment that evening, at about the same time that Rebecca was lying in bed, gazing at the ceiling and smiling to herself, Oliver heard his mobile phone ring and looking at the display it spelled out *Rebecca.*

'Hi Rebecca,' he answered. 'We haven't spoken in a while. I was just thinking of calling you. How are you?'

'I'm fine, Oliver thanks. Actually, though I do need to talk to you.' Rebecca replied in a business-like tone.

'Sure okay, about what?' Oliver asked quizzically.

'I'll come straight out with it,' said Rebecca. 'I don't think we should see each other anymore, it isn't working really if we're honest. I don't think there's any real chemistry between us truthfully. I like you Oliver and I value your help with valuations and so forth, but maybe that's what our relationship should be, a business relationship?'

There she had said it, she had got it all out in one go and she felt slightly light-headed now realising she had spoken fast without breathing. As if by stopping to take a breath she wouldn't be able to get it all out.

There was a pause on the other end of line

'I see, maybe you're right,' Oliver eventually conceded. 'I know I haven't been that attentive just lately. My mind has been elsewhere. You deserve someone who'll be there for you, who'll take care of you. Someone you can trust.'

'That was easy,' thought Rebecca.

Oliver seemed to be taking it much better than she had expected In fact she was astounded just how easy the conversation went and she was relieved.

'But I still hope we can work together, you know… stay friends. I know that sounds like a cliché but I mean it,' Rebecca said with her eyes closed. Lying seemed much easier with her eyes closed.

'Of course we can Rebecca, I'd like that,' he agreed.

'Okay, good. Bye Oliver.'

'Bye Rebecca.'

Oliver ended the call and walked over to the window where he could see the black waters of the Thames flowing out to sea. He searched his contact list and selected another name and placed the call.

'Hello,' said the voice at the other end.

'Alex? It's Oliver here.'

'So she called you I guess?' Asked Alex

'Yes, she did. So tell me, does she trust you now?'

'There's no doubt about it, Oliver. She trusts me completely.'

PART 2

CHAPTER 7

Alex Lewis had been a diligent student and an excellent sportsman in high school. His proud family assumed he would go on to university and continue to play rugby there. Maybe he might even play professionally when he had graduated he was so good at the game. But Alex was a realist and knew that the path to professional sport was not a simple one and anyway he was more interested in what made athletes successful, how they overcame injuries and in the psychology of sport.

He graduated with a fine degree in Physiotherapy and after leaving university he worked hard at several gyms, advising on exercise regimes and nutrition. Soon his skills were noticed elsewhere and adding sports psychology to his skill-set Alex was offered a well-paid position in one at the top sports injury clinics in Manchester.

He quickly gained a reputation, and it wasn't long before an ambitious Alex made a name for himself and set up his own clinic.

Working for yourself is a dream of many, although not as easy as it might seem. Alex discovered that finding and keeping enough clients, along with accountancy, marketing and the administration skills that are required to keep a successful business going, was a challenge.

What he needed was a mentor, and that happened when he met Mrs. Pearson.

Mrs Pearson was a well-healed widow living in the exclusive suburbs of Cheshire. She had been long-term sufferer of Chronic Obstructive Pulmonary Disease, COPD, and a condition which was becoming increasingly acute and extremely debilitating.

Her doctor advised her that physiotherapy may help deliver some relief from the symptoms and he recommended Alex to her.

And so it proved to be that Alex's skill, although not curing the disease, a fact Mrs Pearson knew well enough, did provide much welcome relief from her symptoms.

The pair hit it off as patient and therapist and over time Mrs. Pearson took an interest in Alex's career. She recommended new clients, helped him with an accountant and advised on ways to promote his business.

She saw something in Alex, in the way he came from humble roots and applied himself with hard work and determination, which she didn't see in her own offspring. Her son Marcus was the complete opposite of Alex. A lazy, privileged fool who thought the world owed him a living. He spent his mother's money and rarely came to visit unless he wanted something. Naturally Mrs Pearson took a liking to Alex.

COPD is not a condition that improves and after a few months it became clear that alternative methods would be needed if any decent quality of life could continue. Mrs Pearson had read that using hypnotherapy could provide her with the relief from pain she was seeking.

She paid for Alex to train to add hypnotherapy to his skill-set. As always, Alex was an excellent student and picked up the skill with ease.

Marcus Pearson was becoming increasingly jealous of the close relationship that Alex had developed with his mother. His dirty little mind convinced him something else was going on between them and that Alex was just an attractive toy-boy offering more than physiotherapy and in reality he was only after his mother's money… his money. So Marcus installed a hidden spy camera in his mother's bedroom, spiteful man that he was.

The video gained from the camera showed nothing that could be deemed as inappropriate was going on, how could it? But still he persisted in spying on his mother and Alex in the hope it would change. After several weeks something did change.

Mrs. Pearson's condition was getting no better, despite Alex's best intentions and she knew the pain and suffering of her condition would only get worse. It took a lot of soul searching and agonising thought, but eventually she told Alex of her plan and how she wanted him to help her.

At first Alex was horrified at her proposal; he baulked at the thought of helping her to end her own life.

In Mrs Pearson's case time was not a great healer and over the weeks that followed Alex witnessed her worsening condition. Despite his increased attention to her and the more frequent experimentation with hypnotherapy, in an effort to harness the body's own healing power, Alex could not help but feel despair at the pain she was increasingly suffering. Reluctantly, but with great compassion for the misery his mentor and friend was enduring, Alex agreed to help.

Mrs. Pearson's death was not wholly unexpected, and many said it was a blessed relief for the poor woman. What was unexpected, however, were the contents of the *Last Will & Testament* of Mrs. Phyllis Pearson.

She had bequeathed to Alex all the cash in her various bank accounts, which was a little over £300,000. The house, possessions and her investments, not to mention the life insurance pay-out, were all left to her uncaring son Marcus. But this spoiled rich kid wanted everything.

The meeting at Marcus's lawyer was an acrimonious well planned trap. A video that Marcus had prepared from the spy camera recordings was expertly edited to suggest an inappropriate relationship existed between his mother and Alex. But worse was the insinuation that the use of hypnotherapy was used to persuade his mother to take her own life and ensure that Alex would benefit from her death.

'Assisted suicide is illegal in the United Kingdom,' Alex was told. 'Anyone found to be assisting a suicide can be jailed for up to 14 years, under the Suicide Act 1961.'

Worst still was the suggestion that as Alex had engineered the whole thing for his own ends and by reporting that to the police would mean they could charge Alex with Mrs. Pearson's murder. The video evidence was pretty damning after all.

Of course the whole purpose of the trap was to make Alex give up on his right to any of the money Mrs. Pearson's had bequeathed to him.

That wasn't really a problem for Alex, who was still dealing with the upset of his friend's death, he never expected or wanted anything from her. But it didn't end there. Marcus was so vindictive and jealous of Alex that part of the deal was that he should leave the North-West altogether. He had friends in high places and would make sure Alex never had another client to manipulate.

Alex's life had just fallen apart, but Marcus Pearson was now considerably richer and had more money to waste on buying art. Marcus liked the idea of buying expensive paintings. It would make him appear civilised and acceptable to the rich and famous he yearned to rub shoulders with.

Marcus Pearson and Oliver were like two peas from a pod and although they were acquainted they wouldn't necessarily be called friends. Each would happily cheat the other. So it was with some satisfaction that Oliver happily encouraged Marcus to pay way over the odds for a second piece of abstract art to go with one he had sold him a few months earlier. That first piece Marcus neither understood nor liked, but what did Oliver care when it increased his commission. Not that Marcus cared as he was spending Alex's money.

To help celebrate his latest acquisition, Marcus invited Oliver back to his recently inherited house for drinks and as Marcus got drunker, he couldn't help but brag about how he had scammed Alex out of what was rightfully left to him. He even took great pleasure in sliding a DVD into the player to show Oliver the apparent evidence.

Oliver watched the large TV screen enthralled. He could clearly see Alex touching the woman's body carefully, almost lovingly he thought to himself. He recognised the skill of a physiotherapist at work. Even though there was no sound to accompany the pictures, a twisted view was forming in his mind. However, the scene which excited him most was the one with the woman in the bed.

There was gentleness with which Alex helped the woman into bed, which Oliver interpreted as being sexual, the kiss he gave her reinforcing his fantasy. But the most exciting part was when he watched Alex check the contents of a syringe and carefully inserted it into the woman's arm.

Oliver grinned as he watched Alex slide into bed with the woman, holding her in his arms for what seemed an eternity until he laid her down, rested her head gently on the pillow and kissed her one final time.

Marcus roared with drunken laughter at the end of his little show, took the disc from the machine and threw it toward a wastebasket, missing it completely.

'I won't need that anymore. What an idiot,' he laughed, raising his whiskey glass. 'Thanks for everything mum.'

Oliver eyed the disc lying on the floor. What he had seen not only interested him, it excited him in more way than one. After ensuring that Marcus would pass out drunk, he took the disc and watched it over and over, making plans.

Alex wasn't hard to find and Oliver was so sympathetic to his plight. Yes, he knew Marcus and hated him too. These so-called art lovers were all the same, greedy and selfish. Oliver wanted to give the badly treated man a break just to prove not everyone in the art world was a fraud.

'Don't worry about the cost,' Oliver had told Alex. 'I'll help you get set up in London and we can figure out a way you can pay me back later.'

A way for how Alex could pay him back was already firmly in place in Oliver's mind.

CHAPTER 8

I had to pay an unexpected visit to see mum at the nursing home. By rights everything should have been much better now, not least because of the way I had broken up so painlessly with Oliver. But life isn't like that and much as I wanted to be thinking about Alex, since we'd had the greatest sex ever, things with mum had taken a turn for the worse, so now my focus was elsewhere.

Mum had got another infection which seemed par for the course these days and although the doctor had prescribed antibiotics, her demeanour was not a good one. She spent most of the weekend being belligerent and abusing the staff, using language the likes of which I had never heard her use before. I could not believe that she even knew some words she was yelling even existed.

She wasn't so kind to me either when I went to visit, trying to repair the sensitives of the staff at the care home, although in fairness to them, they didn't appear to be particularly bothered being called bitches. I tried to switch her attention to happier times.

In an effort to help mum feel more at comfortable in the nursing home I had purchased and decorated her room with several framed copies of art by famous, well-known artists that mum also loved, as art had been part of her life from a very young age. I assumed that by surrounding her with colourful paintings her surroundings would be calming and familiar. Art would help her settle and feel more secure in the home.

I'd chosen the famous Van Gogh *Sunflowers,* as mum loved flowers and I placed this strategically above her mantelpiece. The other one from an Italian-Jewish artist called Amedeo Modigliani, which was a landscape piece, entitled *Landscape Southern France* hand painted in 1919. I positioned this next to her bed, to emulate a window whenever she looked at it.

'This is no artist,' she told me pointing to the Van Gogh. 'It's nothing but a fake and a child's painting!'

'Mum, I don't know how you can say that, this was painted by a very famous Dutch painter called Van Gogh, one of the great impressionist artists of his time.' I said to her.

'Nothing but a fake I tell you, he can't even sketch flowers in a vase,' she insisted.

'You don't understand mum, even though the artist was trained to paint classically the impressionists painted in a different way, they were radicals.' I retorted. 'And what about the Modligiani landscape, surely you must like that one?' I asked.

'That one's even worse,' she exclaimed. 'And more of a fake than the flowery one.'

To be honest, I was surprised to hear that mum had such a low opinion of Van Gogh and Modigliani. But what she said next was as shocking as it was unexpected.

'Michelangelo, now he was a genius.' She claimed. 'You know this to be true, Rebecca, just one look at the drawing that Nonno gave me to pass on to you someday proves this. The Leda and the Swan sketch he found was never discovered you know, Nonno made sure of this. Michelangelo's artistry is faultless!'

I was stunned and felt lightheaded momentarily 'Ssssssh mum, keep your voice down,' I pleaded, which was pointless as she was on a roll.

'Nonno found it in the war, risked his own life he did, stopped them getting their hands on it. It's not a fake I can assure you cara. Please make sure nobody finds it won't you? You'll protect it?' She asked.

'Oh dear mum, you certainly know how to make up a story.' I replied.

'Story?' she asked 'This is no story.'

Mum looked at me unblinking and I could see in her eyes the mother who I thought I had lost. It was only for a brief moment, but however brief that moment was, I recognised my mother again.

How about I take you to downstairs to the lounge for a cup of tea and biscuits, I know you like biscuits.' I asked her.

'Ooh yes please,' she replied vacantly again. 'Let's do that.'

So it was true, it was a real Michelangelo. Nonno, my grandfather, and Nonna, my grandmother, had rescued it from the Nazi art thieves. Somehow Robins knew something about this, maybe not the whole story, but he knew something.

Thoughts flashed through my mind about how the family secret had become known by those outside. Robins could only have known about the existence of the drawing from Poppa.

Poppa had always considered himself as an outsider to some degree. Obviously Nonna was a true Italian and my grandpa was an absolute Italophile. His love of Italian art, its culture and its food meant that our household was an Italian household, with mum clearly thinking of herself as Italian as Spaghetti. When Poppa married Mum, he accepted that, but I'm sure he always felt a little bit of a stranger in his own land on occasions.

Maybe it was him who had let something slip whilst having too many glasses of vino. Then I thought of what I had done, foolishly letting Oliver in on the secret, but Oliver and Robins had no connection so it only went to show how secrets will be drawn out, eventually.

Finding the drawing however had been a complete surprise to me, even though it seemed that Robins may have had an inkling.

I never truly accepted Poppa's death as anything less than suspicious. Even the coroner seemed to agree and declared an open verdict. We all knew Poppa drank too much and if it had only been the presence of alcohol in his blood system, then maybe I would have come to terms with it. But the bruises on his body, what were those, how did he get them?

A couple of days after the funeral the family solicitor handed me several things that Poppa had prepared in advance. One of those things was a sealed envelope with the code to the safe in the back office of the gallery and instructions to change the code to one of my own choosing and to keep it secret, known only to myself. When I opened the safe for the first time it was then I spotted the battered box containing the Michelangelo sketch and another sealed envelope on top of it.

I remember the contents of the letter word for word.

My Darling Rebecca,

This was entrusted to your mother, the love of my life, so now I entrust it to you. She never really knew what to do with it and sadly now she is unable to think clearly, but I know you'll know what to do with it when the time is right.

But I had no idea what to do with it and now it seemed trouble had turned up because of it. I felt suddenly alone.

I needed someone I could trust and just then my mobile phone chirped that a text had been received.

It was from Alex.

Hey beautiful

Time for another massage?

I'll even throw in some more hypnotherapy for free again.

Was I pleased to hear back from him? I typed out my reply.

Just what I need if you have time

Alex's reply was instant

I always have time for you

Is tomorrow too soon?
No, it wasn't too soon at all.
C U at 10am xx
Rebecca

I put my phone back in my handbag; at least I have something nice to look forward to again.

'Who was that on your phone?' Mum asked. 'Was it your Poppa? Will he be home soon?'

CHAPTER 9

Oliver and Alex were seated in the consulting room of the Putney offices. For all his size and physical presence Alex seemed agitated and almost intimidated by Oliver.

'What time are you expecting her?' Oliver asked Alex.

'Her appointment is for ten o'clock,' Alex replied.

'Then she'll be here at about half past ten in that case,' sneered Oliver. 'She's never on time for anything. It's one of the things that annoyed me about her. She'll be late for her own funeral.'

'One of the things that annoyed you,' asked Alex. 'How many things are there? I thought you two were an item, or at least used to be.'

Oliver screwed his face up, trying to display a contempt for the woman he had dated on and off for the best part of seven years.

'Well, for starters she has never used the L word towards me, not ever. We only had sex about once a month and that wasn't every month and do you know what? I get the impression that she didn't even like me touching her.'

Alex decided not to comment, he knew that Rebecca wanted him to touch her. He could tell by the way she reacted to him when his hands manipulated her body during the massage. The signs may have been subtle, but he knew, he could tell. And as for sex, it had been so good between them, really good. But he now felt bad

102

that it had ever happened. It would have been much easier for him if it hadn't been that way. Now Alex was trapped. Trapped by Oliver and trapped by the mixed emotions he had for Rebecca.

Who was he really deceiving, Rebecca or himself? Damn the pretentious, self-satisfying, repugnant world of art and the people in it. He tried to remind himself that Rebecca was part of that world, the same one that had caused his current predicament.

Look where being kind had got him. No, he told himself; he would not allow himself to get trapped again. But it still didn't feel right; being deceitful wasn't in his nature.

He'd looked for a way out and found none. Even now, however, Alex still didn't know the truth of Oliver's scheme, although clearly it wasn't good. He needed to know what he was involved in.

'Listen Oliver, I don't know exactly what you want but whatever it is I won't hurt Rebecca.'

'Who said anybody would get hurt?' Oliver replied, 'Oh, unless you're talking about Toby, Mr. Robins'… what should we call him now err, assistant? You hurt him and Mr Robins isn't happy about that.'

'What the hell Oliver, that's the whole problem with whatever is going on here. I turn up at the gallery and there's two shady looking men threatening a woman. What was I supposed to do?'

'That was a stroke of luck for us actually He was just trying it on. All you need to know is this. Rebecca has something that is precious to me, something I need and I know Robins wants it too. Unlike me, Mr. Robins and his organisation will use any means to get their hands on it. I, on the other hand, can get it for him using more peaceful means. I get what I need, he pays me handsomely. I pay you and you get a practice in London just like I promised. Rebecca doesn't get hurt and they harm not a single hair on her pretty head.'

'Won't she call the police when she discovers whatever you're after is missing?'

'No, she won't Alex. She won't, she can't. It's not hers to own in the first place. You just need to get me the codes I need and then we'll all move on.'

'I just hope she falls deep enough under this time,' Alex responded to the vague explanation Oliver had given.

'Well, if she doesn't we'll have to give her another gift certificate won't we Alex?' Oliver retorted smugly.

Alex was about to object to the suggestion when they heard the door to the shop front open and a female shout, 'Hello shop!' and the door slam shut.

Oliver looked at his wristwatch in shock, 'My God she's early.'

Alex hustled Oliver towards the door at the back of the room. 'Quick, upstairs and wait in the flat. I'll come and find you when we're done.'

'Don't forget what I've asked you to do now. You know what I need.' Oliver reminded Alex as he ascended the stairs which led to the small flat above the shop.

'I know, I know. Now hurry and stay up there until it's over.' Closing the door behind him to hide the fact anybody else was in the building. Alex composed himself and stepped through into the unfinished reception to greet an early and excited Rebecca.

'You're early,' Alex said and immediately regretted that he had allowed himself to repeat Oliver's observation about Rebecca's timing.

Rebecca reached up to Alex, wrapping an arm around his neck.

'It's never too early for you. I couldn't sleep thinking about what you're going to do to me.' She offered her lips to his and he could feel the softness of her kiss which far from settling him only made his anxiety even more acute. But sensing no way out of his dilemma, he took her by the hand to lead her through to the treatment room.

'Oh, someone's in a hurry to get me out of my clothes.' Rebecca giggled like a schoolgirl and Alex was feeling concerned that her playfulness this morning would prevent him being successful.

He set the lighting down low and tried to assert an air of calm by turning on the soft gentle music to create just the right ambience.

'Just make yourself comfortable on the table in the same way the last time you were here and I'll be back in a few minutes.'

'Okay,' she responded.

Alex left her in the room and closed the door behind him. How had he got himself into this mess he wondered? It's the greedy, pretentious, self-serving world of the art dealer, that's how. He tried to concentrate on the fact that Rebecca was part of that world. All he had to do was to complete the task assigned to him and he would be free of them all. Free to get on with his life.

'I'm ready,' He heard a cheerful Rebecca shout to him from the treatment room next door.

Alex studied Rebecca's body stretched on the massage table in front of him. The crisp white sheet draped across her back, showing her naked shoulders. He approached the table to adjust the sheet and fold it further down her back. As he lifted the sheet he glimpsed more than he had intended and could see that she was completely naked. Rebecca's shoulders shook, and he knew she was laughing, amused at how she had surprised him.

Alex feared her mischievous behaviour may make his task more difficult, so he would need all of his skills this morning.

He applied the oil to his hands, rubbing it in thoroughly to cover each finger, making sure the liquid upon them would be warm when he placed them on Rebecca's body. His first touch was gentle and slow and he felt her shoulders relax under the caress of his hands. With unhurried deliberate movements Alex worked the muscles in Rebecca's sides, her back and then her shoulders where the tension had long since disappeared. This gave proof to his skill as a masseuse. He could also tell that Rebecca was relaxing under his mastery, but even so, Alex was all too aware that to rush things now would undo all of his good work and his main aim for Rebecca.

Alex's warm hands followed the contours of Rebecca's smooth body. His hands moved down from her neck and shoulders to her sides, soothing, stroking, his hands never leaving her body.

Carefully Alex was ensuring Rebecca entered a state of deep relaxation, even the sound of mesmerising eastern music, the sounds of nature and water gently trickling helped create the mood he sought for his purpose.

He could tell that she was becoming more and more relaxed, losing the agitation she possessed when she had arrived. Alex noticed how her breathing became slow, deep and steady so he knew it was time to talk.

Alex used a voice which was low, deep and soothing which complimented the tenderness of his touch. 'Relax deeper now,' he urged. 'Breathe in…. and breathe out, slowly, gently. Allow yourself to drift into a deeper state of relaxation.'

As before, he encouraged Rebecca to imagine that she was resting in her favourite place in nature, alone in the sun in the warmest and quietest of days. His calming voice persuaded her to believe that she could actually feel the heat of the sun's rays on her skin. He described how each limb felt in the warmth of the summer sun and how each part of her body was rested and how peaceful she felt as she lay there.

Alex needed her to enter a deeper state of relaxation and he knew Rebecca could. He had proved that during their first hypnotic encounter. So he began to describe the day drawing to a close and night-time falling, which would associate the image with her feelings of sleep and relaxation.

'The sun is descending as evening approaches and the sky is ablaze with colour. Shades of gold, red and orange and now the sun itself disappears over the horizon little by little until darkness falls over you. It's perfectly still, it's a quiet, beautiful night and you're fast asleep.'

But even then Alex knew he needed to take her sub-conscious mind deeper and deeper. Alex was an expert at his craft and he took Rebecca's mind on a journey down into new levels of altered consciousness.

He encouraged Rebecca to believe that she was floating up, weightless into the night sky, drifting over the earth below her and then bringing her down again to earth as daylight reappeared. Now the feeling of descending was planted in her mind. Down and further down as the pictures and scenes he was creating compelled her subconscious mind to also go down, go deeper. Once more Alex painted an image of the beautiful, peaceful garden and yet he knew he needed to take her deeper still.

All the time Alex's voice remained smooth, calm and compelling. He didn't rush or hurry the process; he knew this was vital. He was a master of his skill, painting pictures in Rebecca's mind with his words.

Alex's next picture brought her to staircases which lead to the beach where he had previously taken her to in her imagination. Each step represented a deeper level of consciousness.

'You want to go down to the beach Rebecca and these ten steps will take you there. As you go down each step, you will feel even more relaxed. You will drift deeper and deeper into a wonderful state of sleep but you will still hear my voice. I will count as we go down the steps… one, sleepier. Two, even more tired.'

And so he continued with each step until at the bottom of the staircase.

'Ten and you are at the very bottom. Fast asleep, but your subconscious mind is open to new ideas, new suggestions and you want to go to the beach because I am waiting for you there and you trust me.'

Alex watched Rebecca's body, looking for the tell-tale signs which would show that she was where he wanted her to be.

'There's a gate for you to open to meet me at the beach. It's a high metal gate with solid bars. There's no way around it or over it, but the gate is locked Rebecca. It's locked on my side and I want to be with you, to touch you, to hold you in my arms and kiss you my darling. Do you want that too?'

After a few seconds which caused Alex's heartbeat to quicken, 'Yes,' came Rebecca's softly spoken, automaton like reply.

'Good girl,' Alex continued. 'The lock is exactly the same as the lock on your safe, it has the same combination. If you tell me the combination, I can open the gate and you can come through to me. What is the combination Rebecca?'

Rebecca made no reply and the silence caused Alex's heart to race again and for a moment he was he almost panicked that his plan was about to fail. But he calmed his own breathing, just as Rebecca's was calm, and proceeded to deepen her trance and her desire.

'If you help me open the gate, we can be together. I want to lift you up and carry you to a private, secret place in the soft sand dunes far away from this gate which is keeping us apart. There we can lie down together in the warm sunlight and we can make love. But you need to give me the code so we can do that or we will kept apart and you can't be with me. What's the code Rebecca, you can tell me, you want to tell me don't you?'

Slowly but willingly Rebecca recited to three sets of numbers of the safe combination Alex desperately needed. 'Twenty-five, sixty-two, forty-seven.'

Alex jotted the numbers down on a pad he had placed nearby in the hope of success. He studied Rebecca as she lay still and silent, her breathing deep, slow and steady. Pleased with his skill but troubled by his use of them, the hypnosis continued.

'The gate is open now Rebecca, come through to me my darling and let me carry you in my arms to our secret place where we can be together at last. As I carry you, you begin to feel light and it's as if you are floating on air. You feel so peaceful and happy as I lay you down on the soft sand, where the warmth of the sun on your skin makes you feel so very tired and sleepy.'

Alex studied Rebecca lying still and peaceful on the table. She looked so calm, so serene, which was exactly as he had intended.

He lifted the sheet which was barely covering her waist and looked at the beauty of her naked body. Alex hesitated for a moment, lost in his discovery, then felt shame at himself for staring in her defenseless state. He quickly covered her shoulders, smoothing out the ripples of the fabric gently with his hands and softly tucking the white material around her motionless body.

'And now you notice comfortable sun-bed set out for you to relax on,' Alex explained to her. 'It's the most comfortable sun bed ever and you can't resist lying on it. It's so soft that all you want to do is lie down and sleep in the warm sun.' His melodic voice persuading Rebecca's deep subconscious to sink ever deeper into the hypnotic trance. Confident that he had succeeded in what they demanded of him, Alex gently bent over Rebecca's body and kissed her gently on her back.

He realised his work was nearly over, but he also knew that he couldn't possibly see Rebecca again after what he had just done. He had allowed himself to be used in the worst possible way, using his power against a woman they meant him to detest but found he was having feelings for. It wasn't meant to be this way.

Exactly what he would do next, Alex wasn't sure. All he knew was, he needed to leave London and do so soon.

He picked up Rebecca's handbag and gingerly crept toward the door, opening it as quietly as he could and taking great care not to wake the sleeping Rebecca.

Oliver sat waiting for him, grinning like a Cheshire car. 'You really are very good at this aren't you Alex? I almost thought I was on that beach for a moment. Hey, I bet you could get her to do absolutely anything you wanted her to do. I'm not sure why I asked you to get the safe combination at all. Maybe it would have been simpler just for you to hypnotise her and tell her to hand the drawing over to me?'

'I've already explained to you it doesn't work that way. It's about a heightened state of imagination not about getting the subject to do things.'

'Maybe it is, but I've seen Stage Hypnotists make people bark like dogs or think they're Queen Victoria. You should think about giving up the therapy business and consider show business instead. Of course you'd have to give up fondling women's bodies if you did that.

112

Tough call hey?' Oliver laughed at his teasing of Alex.

Oliver had Alex right where he wanted him and now he could see that his own deceptive plan was coming together. He smiled as he thought of his own cunning skills.

Alex made no comment to Oliver's joke, instead he opened Rebecca's hand-bag and took out a bunch of keys which he handed to Oliver, who removed the ones he needed from the keyring. He placed them flat on a clean, white sheet of paper spread out on the desk. With his mobile phone Oliver proceeded to take a series of close-up photographs of each key.

'It's amazing what you can do with a few photographs these days if you know the right people.' Oliver gloated handing the keys back to Alex. 'Have you something else for me?' He asked.

Alex handed him a slip of paper which he had written the combination Rebecca had revealed to him on.

'And the other code?' Oliver asked Alex.

'What other code?'

'The code to the gallery alarm. It's no good having the door keys to the gallery and the safe combination if as soon as I open the door the alarm alerts every Bobby in London is it?'

'I don't have that, you only asked me to get you the safe combination, and that's what I've done for you. You get the damned alarm code yourself, after all she used to be your girlfriend or didn't she trust you that much?'

Oliver looked annoyed. He always felt that Rebecca didn't trust him and he had just witnessed how Alex had made it seem so easy for her to trust him 'No I guess dear sweet Rebecca didn't trust me at all, which makes all this so much more enjoyable. No-one is good enough for her, or so she thinks. She isn't such a catch anyway, the middle class nobody. Now go back in there and use your undoubted talents to get the bitch to tell you the alarm code.'

'No, Oliver that won't work, she's in a different state now. The process needs to be started all over again and anyway she's getting too used to hypnotism and if I try this too often and it doesn't work, she'll know something isn't right.' Alex lied through his teeth, but he knew Oliver's knowledge of hypnotism was non-existent so he could say anything to confuse him.

'Maybe there are other ways to discover the code?' Suggested Oliver. 'Maybe Robins' men could get it out of her?'

Alex panicked and said the first thing that came into his head. 'There's no need for that, I'll call round to the gallery just before she closes up tomorrow and I'll find a way to get the code for you. But after that I'm done and you give me all the copies of the video you have of me.'

'That wasn't so hard was it? A good old-fashioned bit of snooping and you won't even need to get her to take her clothes off for you. Thinking of which, is she naked in there? How about a quick photograph for me to remember her by?'

114

Alex barred his way into the treatment room.

'She'll wake up and it will ruin the whole thing.'

'Oh well, she's not all that anyway. I can have my pick of women when Robins pays me off and you'll do okay too Alex. £100,000 for your part in all this will set you up nicely don't you think?'

Oliver's smugness made Alex's blood boil, but he knew he was powerless to do anything about it. As long as nobody gets hurt, he told himself, these arty types are all crooks anyway he reasoned and Rebecca was wrapped up with the lot of them. She chose this life; she chose this world, a world that had reduced him to this. It had reduced him to a con-man.

But try as he might, Alex couldn't reconcile what he had done to Rebecca. He had lied to her in the most dreadful way.

Smug Oliver left the building feeling like the cat that got the cream and Alex returned to where Rebecca lay. He studied her resting body for a few moments, lost in thought. Then slowly he awoke her from her deep trance, instructing her to forget everything that had happened during her hypnosis.

CHAPTER 10

The new season's art catalogue was overdue and the events of the last few weeks had distracted my efforts. I needed to make some money again and if I was to meet my deadlines I needed to crack on and get the job done, starting with asking my usual catalogue printer to visit the gallery to discuss the various pieces of art that I had for sale.

Phillip, an expert printer and art photographer, had spent most of the day in the gallery with me compiling a list of everything I wanted to put in the catalogue. Phillip had already photographed most of the pieces in his studio under proper lighting conditions, but I had a few pieces he needed to take away with him.

In fact, it was a busy day in the gallery as I also had an electrician in, doing some work for me, one of them being to ensure the down-lights over the paintings was correct. After all, if I was preparing for a sale then everything had to look perfect. He was just packing his tools to leave, when the bell above the door announced another visitor to the gallery. It was Alex.

'Hi Alex, I didn't expect to see you today.' I said, greeting him with a quick kiss on his soft lips.

From the corner of my eye I noticed that Lucy was watching our interaction with interest and was that a sly smile I saw on her face?

'My, it's busy in here today,' he observed, seeing Phillip and the electrician scurrying about.

'I need to earn some money, Alex,' I told him. 'Girls don't just want to have fun you know. Some of them have to work.'

Continuing to inspect everything I had asked the electrician to do was I as asked, I signed his worksheet to show my satisfaction; he gathered up his tool bag and equipment and left. I walked about the gallery, checking each painting that hung on the walls and that the gallery was clean and tidy. Alex followed me around silently, always about a pace or two behind me but saying nothing. He seemed on edge somehow.

'So what brings you here today,' I asked him.

'Oh nothing really,' he replied nonchalantly. 'I was in the area and I thought I would just call in to see my favourite client.'

'Favourite… is that because I'm your only client,' I joked.

Alex managed a wry smile and Lucy, who was looking over the top of a clipboard she held in front of her face, winked at me.

After a few minutes of him following me around in silence, Alex finally spoke. 'I was wondering how you were feeling today… you know… after yesterday's session?'

Lucy's eyes opened wide over the top of the clipboard.

'I feel wonderful,' I replied truthfully. 'All those aches and pains have gone and I'm feeling a little more relaxed about things now.' I looked at Lucy's enquiring face and with hands on my hips answered her unspoken question. 'Physiotherapy Lucy if you must know.'

Lucy raised one quizzical eyebrow. 'If you say so.'

Alex appeared satisfied with my answer but still somewhat edgy.

'Excuse me for a few moments Alex,' I said. 'I still have some things to discuss with Phillip and after that I'll give you my full attention.'

'That's fine, sure,' he replied, 'I didn't mean to interrupt.'

He wandered around the gallery looking at the paintings, but not really looking if you get my drift. Lucy watched him intently with a wicked smirk on her face. I could tell that Alex was aware of her interest in him and that he was doing his best to ignore her.

'Do you like art,' Lucy eventually asked him.

'I don't really know much about it,' Alex responded. 'I think it's all lost on me I'm afraid.'

'But I bet you know what you like don't you Alex?' Lucy teased as Lucy is fond of doing. 'I know what I'd like.'

Alex blushed. As I have said before, Lucy is a law unto herself and no man is safe around her. Any other woman would have been jealous, but I knew that Lucy was just playing with him to amuse herself. It amused me too. However, there was work to be done and so I continued to discuss my requirements with Phillip until the gallery door was opened yet again and Oliver stepped inside. Lucy's demeanour changed immediately from smiles to scowls.

118

To be honest, Oliver was the last person I had expected to see. 'I'll be with you in a minute,' I told him, frustrated that my time was being interrupted so.

'No problem,' said Oliver. 'Hi Alex,' and he walked over to chat with his partner. They stood together in the corner and talked in low tones, their backs turned against us as if they didn't want anyone to hear what they were discussing. It was almost conspiratorial you could say.

'I'd love to know what those two have to discuss,' I thought.

'It's getting too crowded in here,' Lucy suddenly announced, slipping her coat on 'I'd better be off, see you tomorrow Rebecca.'

'Bye Lucy, I'll see you tomorrow.' And with that she was gone.

After a short while I wrapped up my dealings with Phillip and turned my attention to Oliver 'So, what brings you here?' I asked.

'Well Rebecca, I have a client who is looking for a buyer for a painting he has. He needs to raise some funds quickly and I wondered if you'd be interested. I thought I'd ask before I ask around my other contacts. Look, I've got a photograph.' Oliver explains, taking a glossy photograph out of his bag to show me. 'What do you think?'

'Let's have a look. Hmm, I'm not sure about this one. Abstract art isn't really my field. What do you think Phillip?'

Phillip glanced at the photograph. 'Who took this?' He asked

'I did,' said Oliver.

'With a mobile phone?'

'Yes.'

'You can't really expect anyone to buy an expensive piece of art based this.'

'Sorry but I'm no expert photographer.'

'I can see that. Such a thing needs to be taken in a well-lit studio with proper equipment. Something of value, if this is such a thing, deserves that at least don't you think?'

Phillip was chastising Oliver for his amateur approach and I could see Oliver balk at the implication that he was not a professional. It was strange because Oliver was a professional. He may be many other things, but he was not an amateur when it came to art and Phillip's words seem to have struck a nerve.

I turned to Phillip to relieve the tension and wrap up the day's events. It was also getting late and time to close up for the day.

'Okay Phillip, thanks for coming today and if you can let me have a costing as soon as possible that would be great. Of course, you'll let me know if everything I've asked for is okay won't you?'

'Of course Rebecca, I don't see a problem there. I'll speak to you tomorrow.'

Phillip collected his things and picked up the portfolio case that held the items he was taking back to his studio. I opened the door for him and Phillip left me alone with Oliver and Alex.

'Okay you two it's been a long day and I want to close up.'

'I've got to run anyway.' said Oliver. He moved forward, placing his hands on my shoulders to kiss me on the cheek, which I offered to him more out of habit than anything else. Actually, he made my skin crawl.

'Right, you too Alex, I need to lock up.'

'Err, okay… I'll just wait for you to lock up properly,' replied Alex, not moving

'Come on, shoo, out with you. I need to set the alarm first.'

He seemed reluctant to step outside into the street, but eventually he did so and I set the code for the alarm.

Alex held the door for me and as I did so it was his turn to kiss me goodbye. He leaned in to kiss me on the cheek but I took his face in my hands and looked at him momentarily then planted my lips to his. Maybe the kiss was too long, maybe not long enough?

'I'll call you?' He asked.

'Not if I call you first.' My reply back, jokingly.

'I hope your mum's feeling better.'

'Me too, I've enough going on right now.'

I watched Alex go; he looked very good from behind. And I thought about men from my past. What is it about men walking away from me? Would this man do the same?

***

When I was a little girl, many of the Italian family's in our part of London, including our little Anglo-Italian family, used to get together for dances, barbeques and other social events. These families all knew each other and in one family in particular there was a really special boy who I liked tremendously.

Roberto had been a part of my life for as long as I could remember and when we became teenagers everyone assumed we would be a proper couple, romantically involved. You know... boyfriend and girlfriend.

He had grown into a real charmer, as Italian men are inclined to be. He was quite tall which is unusual. Most of the other men that I knew from the Italian community barely reached five foot six inches, so I'd always had to wear my flats if I went out with any of them.

I hate flat shoes; I love a shoe with a high, thin heel. They make your legs look slimmer and longer. They also help make you look taller too, which is no bad thing. With Roberto I could wear such a shoe and we looked great together.

He dressed stylishly, was well groomed and he too loved shoes. His were always of the finest Italian leather. However, I wasn't the only women attracted to him, so it made me feel quite special that he'd chosen me for his girlfriend.

We enjoyed a great relationship and my family loved him. Mum invited him for dinner all the time and Roberto would help her wash up at the end of the meal and bring Poppa a bottle of wine. They loved him. I loved him. Everybody loved Roberto.

I was only twenty-one when he suggested we get engaged, which came as a surprise because

I was at university at the time and we didn't see each other every weekend. But it still seemed the right thing to do. My third year at university was in Italy, which meant we would probably not see each other as much, but we thought it would still work. I'd leave for Rome in the September and be back for Christmas and Easter holidays. No problem.

It made me feel guilty sometimes that my mind wasn't focused entirely on Roberto whilst I was enjoying myself in Rome, but that guilt was cut short with an email from my friend Louise. And the email started with the sentence, "*I think there is something you should know.*"

Why do people say, I think there is something you should know, as if they think they're doing you some sort of favour? I usually find what they really mean is; I know something you don't and this news is going to hurt.

Her news was, she had seen Roberto out and about with another woman and they appeared to be more than just friends. I'm not sure if she had great fun revealing that news to me, but I had to know the truth.

I went back to London that same weekend, without announcing it to anyone, and visited all the usual places we would go. I found them at *Spinning 45s*, which was our favourite place to go dancing. Oh yes, they were definitely more than friends, he had his hands all over her backside and she had her tongue so far down his throat, I thought he would choke. I watched them through two whole dances and eventually he saw

123

me staring at them. I thought he might come charging over to plead with me, but he was a coward and tried to pretend he hadn't seen me. And worst still, the woman he was with was my best friend Janelle.

Janelle and I hit it off at university and we went everywhere together. We seemed to have so much in common, not only an interest in art but in music, books, clothes and so it seemed, in Roberto. To add insult to injury, I learned that the pair of them began their shameless behaviour during the weekend I invited Roberto up to university to have a little fun. Clearly Roberto had lots of fun. Why I didn't recognise it at the time, I'll never know.

Maybe he did me a favour, did I really want to get engaged at twenty-one? I guess I'll never know that either, but it hurt nevertheless. I thought Roberto was The One, except he wasn't, was he?

When I came back for my final year and graduation in England, Oliver was a tower of strength. We shared a lot of common interests and he was never pushy about what our relationship was, or what he expected of me. At the time I needed a friend and Oliver was just that. He was kind then. What has happened since I wonder?

I went back to Rome to study for my Masters and we lost touch until we met by chance in New York.

How did I get over Roberto during my final few months in Rome? One word… shopping.

Lovely, fabulous, brand new clothes. No matter how many I bought, I never grew tired of shopping and how it made me feel. I couldn't really afford it on a student's budget. I figured I would ask Poppa to help me out with the credit card bills, the credit card he gave me to help with emergencies whilst I was away from home and this was definitely an emergency.

New clothes helped fill the void within me, at least for a brief time anyway. I could always make myself feel ten feet tall and oh so good just by spending cash (or Poppa's credit card) on something fabulous.

To compensate for all the badness, I loved the thrill of shopping to make myself look and feel better, sexier, slimmer even. It soon became a constant compulsive drive for me to help put those ugly emotions to bed.

Living and studying in Italy made it even easier too. My Italian girlfriends had this wonderful gift of bartering for everything in every shop they went in. Even designer brands such as Dolce and Gabbana, Versace and Armani were not immune from their powers of negotiation. I had such fun walking into stores and watching them slip into gear.

They would encourage me to try on practically everything in the shop. The poor assistants would end up fraught, exhausted and totally frustrated. Even though I'd made my choice long ago, my friends would give me the wink and ask what the price the garment was, despite there being a label on it. Suddenly, they'd act all alarmed and shocked, order me to take the dress, skirt or top off, claiming they had seen a better garment elsewhere for half the price.

The purpose of these dramatic scenes was to persuade the assistant, who was dying to make a sale, to give me the biggest discount possible. I've never been able to achieve this myself back home, but in Rome I ended up with the biggest wardrobe of designer clothes imaginable. When it was time to return to London I had so much stuff that I needed to get them all shipped over specially. Another bill Poppa begrudgingly paid for.

I still have most of these clothes; some still with the price tags on having never been worn. They sit on rails in my spare bedroom. I can't seem to part with them, although most probably don't fit me now. They will again one day, I tell myself, after I've lost a few pounds.

Men, who needs a man when you have nice shoes and designer clothes?

***

I congratulated myself on a job well done. I had been very busy and was pleased with the progress I had made in the gallery. I had told Alex I was going to visit my mother, but that wasn't true. Sometimes a girl doesn't want to be around men but she does want to have fun. Sometimes a night out with the girls is just the tonic that's needed and tonight is one of those nights. I made a few phone calls to several friends and hey presto we're in business. My old friend Louise said yes, and she asked if her friend Annie could come along too.

'The more the merrier.' I told her.

Next I called Chloe, Veronica and Sarah and just for the hell of it I thought, why not ask Lucy?

The thing about Lucy is, age is no barrier to her and why should it be? Just because Lucy is 50 something doesn't mean she couldn't have a good time. I knew if Lucy came we'd all have a great time.

When girls want to have a good time, then dancing is a must and so we all agreed that Spinning 45s was the place to go. Yes, my old disco day's venue was still in business.

Disco classics and cheap vodka, okay, maybe vodka isn't cheap but there would be plenty of disco classics.

We literally fell into the place because we'd all met round at Louise's place beforehand and she's plied us with several bottles of Prosecco, so we were well and truly up for a good night.

Handbags on the floor, we formed a tight circle which was closed off to any man who tried to come between us in our wild abandonment.

We danced, we drank, we danced some more. We danced until our feet hurt and of course they hurt because Gucci sling backs with four and half inch heels aren't designed for dancing. But as any woman knows, it's style over function always.

Of course the odd man tried to break our circle, or at least get close. One persistent guy, who really didn't belong in the club, was insistent on dancing as close as he dared to Lucy. What a very foolish man. He looked like he was probably some sort of sales-rep, away from home on business, thinking his ridiculous moves would enable him to get lucky. His luck changed abruptly when they played the Eurhythmic's, *Sisters Are Doin' it for Themselves,* when she turned and sang right in his face at full volume,

'Sisters are doin' it for themselves, standing on their own two feet and ringing on their own bells.'

We, of course, all joined in with the chorus; given that it's a classic that all of the girls loved.

'Sisters are doin' it for themselves!'

We eventually collapsed into one of the seating booths where more Prosecco was ordered because we could all see that Lucy was determined to enjoy herself the most, which was immensely entertaining.

We'd noticed an adjacent booth where a group of boys, who were probably in their late-twenties, early thirties, had been watching us all evening. One in particular had caught Lucy's eye or I should say she had her eye on him and repeatedly beckoned him to come over to join us. I felt sorry for the lad who looked terrified.

When he didn't respond to Lucy's invitation, she went over to join him, sitting as close as possible to the poor boy who was forced to move over and make room for her.

We watched with eager anticipation as to what would happen next. We couldn't hear what Lucy was saying, but we knew from her body language that this boy was onto a sure thing. Clearly petrified by a woman of Lucy's experience it wasn't long before we all saw the object of Lucy's desire make some form of excuse and fled, post-haste, followed by his entourage of friends, who were all laughing at him.

We were all in hysterics and as Lucy returned to us she looked a little perplexed.

'Am I really that frightening?' She laughed.

'Yes, you terrify us.' We all agreed.

This small hiccup would not stop Lucy or the rest of the girls, they were fired up for a night of excitement.

But a sobering thought struck me. What was it I felt for Alex? Did he feel anything for me? So without saying anything I left the group and called an Uber. I had to know, and I had to know now.

CHAPTER 11

Alex thought it was a cliché' that the East End underworld operated out of old Victorian warehouses or dilapidated lock-ups, but as Oliver drew up outside a line of shabby looking railway arch businesses, he realised the cliché' was a reality.

Oliver thumped on the wooden door of an anonymous archway and they could hear sliding bolts on the inside. After a few moments a small door was fractionally opened and an unshaven man in overalls peered at the two men outside. The unshaven man nodded and opened the door fully, allowing Alex and Oliver to step inside.

The ordinary looking exterior of the archway belied the activity inside. Several high-end, executive cars, in various states of build, were crammed into the makeshift workshop. Alex recognised two BMWs, one with its seats removed and the other with its bonnet up and the sparks flying, as a man in protective goggles, applied an angle grinder to the engine. He also spotted a Mercedes and a large red 4x4 partially covered with a dust sheet.

Two burly men in dark suits stood idly by, watching the others working on the cars.

When they noticed Oliver with Alex, one of them grunted, 'this way,' and gestured with a jerk of his head to a glass-partitioned office in the workshop's corner. The men waited for Alex and

Oliver to walk toward the office and fell in behind them to make sure they continued as directed.

One of the men shoved Alex into the back to make him walk quicker. Alex tensed and resisted the urge to push the man back in return. He knew they heavily outnumbered him. Instead, he joked in his best, laid back voice.

'You can go first if you're in a rush.'

'Shut up and just keep going,' was the reply from the Pushy Guy.

'Yeah, hurry up,' added his partner, 'Mr. Robins wants a word with you.'

'He'll want more than just a word,' laughed the Pushy Guy.

'Oh, is that two words then?' asked Alex.

'What?' asked a confused Pushy Guy.

'You know, more than just a word would be two words wouldn't it? I have two words I'd like to say to you,' Alex said in a low voice, but still loud enough to me heard.

'Keep walking,' with another hard shove in Alex's back.

'No, not those two words,' responded Alex, though, keeping his cool. 'But the ones I am thinking of have a similar meaning.'

'Stop antagonising them,' Oliver snapped at Alex, more in fear than anything else. Oliver wasn't sure why they had been summoned either and he wasn't feeling as brave as Alex in the company of the two thugs.

Alex couldn't resist one more taunt at their escorts and he stopped dead in his tracks, squaring up to one doing the pushing and their faces now just millimetres apart.

'I'm only having a bit of fun. I can't believe your mother didn't bring him you up to be genuinely rude and go around shoving people, did she now?'

Alex met his eyes with an unblinking stare and there was a moment of threatening silence until the thinner man interjected.

'Pack it in you two; we can't keep Mr. Robins waiting. Now inside all of you,' he commanded opening the office door.

The four men filed inside, wary of each other. Robins sat at a desk in the corner of an untidy office. Boxes of car parts were stacked against one wall underneath a Pirelli calendar from 2003 with a semi-naked girl accompanying the month. Behind Robins, Alex noted the thick-set man from the day at the gallery.

'Gentlemen, welcome to the transport side of my business,' Robins announced with his arms spread wide in mock greeting.

'Of course this is only one of my business interests, but I thought it best to meet here. No chance of being overhead when we discuss our business I think.'

'No, not here Mr. Robins sir,' chuckled the Pushy Guy who now stood blocking the door. No-one was going anywhere in a hurry, that much was clear.

Oliver was keen to move things on from the palpable tension that hung in the air.

132

'I thought we had an agreement that I would get hold of the Michelangelo drawing for us Mr. Robins, so I must object to you threatening Rebecca. It didn't work with her father and it certainly won't work with her. I should know.'

Pieces were falling into place for Alex. Oliver's scheme was to steal a drawing from Rebecca's safe and this was a much bigger affair than he had been made aware of. He realised for the first time the real danger Rebecca was now in.

Robins smiled, leaning back in his chair interlocking the fingers of his chubby hands together forming steeples with his thumbs. Alex noticed how his fingernails were manicured and neat. He obviously doesn't believe in getting his hands dirty thought Alex.

'Surely you can't blame me for trying Oliver can you? I'm a businessman. It might have worked and that way I get the drawing for a song, compared to the half a million pounds I promised you.' Robins explained cheerfully.

Half a million was also news to Alex and now he understood the real motivation behind Oliver's design on Rebecca and the reason for the blackmail forcing him to help.

'Well, no harm done perhaps,' Oliver replied peevishly. 'We're almost ready to take possession of the drawing and actually the little altercation in Rebecca's gallery played into our hands. Alex's timely arrival and his err, how can I put it, interjection only made her trust him more.'

Robins leant forward onto his desk again. 'Yes, we'll come onto that in a second. What do you mean you're almost ready to take possession? My patience will only be tested so far Oliver.'

Oliver swallowed hard. He knew that wasn't a veiled threat. Robins had a violent reputation. 'We now have the code to the safe and I know she keeps it locked up in there. All we need now is the code to the alarm system.'

'We can just break in and take it then Boss,' said the thickset man, speaking for the first time.

'No, we don't want to do that, we'll have the old Bill swarming all over the place before we're in and out. So how and when are we going to get the alarm code Oliver?'

'Alex will get that for us, won't you Alex? As I've told you, we have the safe code and Rebecca trusts Alex, we're sure we'll have that code very soon.'

Again Robins smiled his creepy smile. 'Oh, I'm sure Alex will get everything he wants from dear Rebecca. Does she lie there and do everything you want her to do for Alex? Is she putty in your hands?'

His three thugs laughed obligingly at their boss's joke.

'Yeah, I bet it's the only way he can get a woman. He's a pervert,' sneered the thickset man.

The look of hatred in his eyes towards Alex was a testament to the fact that there was unfinished business between them. The other two heavies laughed along with their colleague's jibe.

'Okay enough frivolity,' ordered Robins and the room fell silent. 'I've waited a long time to get my hands on that drawing and I'm getting just a little impatient now and believe me gentlemen, you won't it when I get impatient.'

His employees nodded in stern agreement. Oliver's face was white with fear but Alex was continuing to glare at his adversary, his own face fearless in the way an expert poker player would conceal their hand and so concealing his thoughts and feelings towards the man.

'So you've got the safe code as you said you would but your promised to get in and out of the gallery undetected and I fear that is making me just a little impatient now. I've waited long enough, I think, don't you?'

Oliver looked even more uncomfortable than ever. He felt all eyes were on him and the confines of the small office provided a feeling of intense claustrophobia adding to his sense of fear.

Robins leant back in his chair and folded his arms under his chest to convey his impending frustration at Oliver's lack of progress. 'Well, so how are you going to resolve this? I'm waiting.'

'Alex will get the alarm code for us, won't you Alex? Rebecca trusts him completely and he's assured me it's not a problem for him.'

All eyes then turned to Alex and Robins returned to leaning forward on his desk, pushing aside a pile of papers and resting his arms on the cleared space. 'Rebecca trusts Alex completely, I'm pleased to hear that Oliver. I have to admit I had my doubts about what you said was possible, but I'm impressed.'

A little colour returned to Oliver's cheeks and he allowed himself a slight smile.

'But I still need to be sure you'll deliver the final piece of your puzzle.'

The colour drained from Oliver's face once again.

'I'm pleased that our previous meeting at the gallery obviously helped convince Rebecca you really are her knight in shining armour, but I can't help but feel you were maybe a little too enthusiastic in that altercation with Toby here,' said Robins over his shoulder to the thickset man.

'So he's Toby is he,' thought Alex?

The two men continued to glare at each other and the tension between them filled the room with a sense of violence.

'He's just an ugly fat, clumsy oaf,' Alex replied calmly. 'He fell over his own big feet as I seem to recall.'

Toby did not look amused by Alex's remarks but said nothing. He knew this was not the time to interrupt his boss.

Robins rested his chin in his hands, cocked his head to one side and grinned again. 'I like you Alex, really I do. You're fit, athletic and fearless.' Then suddenly, without warning, the friendly voice changed in a snap to that of a ruthless angry man. 'But don't screw with me boy, I won't be messed about by you or anybody. I get what I want and I'll use any method I can to do so.'

An angry Robins then nodded to the two hence-men that had escorted Oliver and Alex into the room. They moved forward quickly, already primed on what their task was. Forcefully the men dragged Alex back to the brick wall at the end of the office and held him there. Alex was strong, but not strong enough to overcome the pair.

Toby removed his jacket and rolled up his shirtsleeves as he walked round from behind Robins who was calm again now. Toby directed his attention to Alex.

'You'll get that code and you'll get it for me by the end of the week otherwise Toby and the boys will get it for me and something tells me you wouldn't want that.' Robins looked up at Toby who was still adjusting his shirt sleeves. 'Show young Alex here how we like to persuade people, will you Toby? Oh, but be sure not to mark his pretty face. We wouldn't want Rebecca to be frightened off now, would we?'

Alex knew what was coming. He considered using his feet and giving as good as he was about to get, but he knew he was out-numbered and would never be able to beat all of them. He tensed every muscle in his abdomen awaiting the first blow.

Alex's muscles were strong and honed through his constant workouts, but even so he could not fully overcome the searing hot pain he felt when Toby's fist crashed into his stomach. Alex fought to control the air escaping from his lungs as the blows continued. Despite the pain Alex knew he was younger and fitter than Toby and tried to hang on, waiting for Toby to tire. Each punch hurt like hell and he wondered how long he could resist.

'Enough,' shouted Robins and Alex was dropped to the floor where he attempted to recover his breath, each new intake bringing fresh pains. 'Get them out,' Robins instructed. 'And remember Oliver, the end of the week unless you want to see what else my boys can do.'

Alex shook off the hands that tried to lift him up; he was determined to hold on to his dignity as he tidied his clothing and followed Oliver out of the building. He wanted to lean on Oliver but resisted, despite the agony he felt from each breath he took, Alex valiantly strode out head held as high as he was able.

He struggled to lower himself into the car where Oliver spoke for the first time.

'You've got to get that alarm code Alex. We can't afford to upset Robins any further. Please say you'll persuade Rebecca, for all our sakes?'

Alex didn't reply. He sat rubbing his bruised torso, knowing that his dealings with Toby were not at an end.

CHAPTER 12

The Uber dropped me outside the front of Alex's studio; I knew he lived above the shop. I couldn't see a doorbell; I hate people who don't have doorbells on their front doors. How was I supposed to attract his attention? I banged on the door as a couple came out of the restaurant next door and gave me strange looks.

'What are you looking at? Can't you see I'm desperate for some physio?'

They moved away thinking I was a lunatic or drunk. Perhaps I was both? I banged on the door again and stepped back to see if there were any lights on upstairs I could see that there was, so I sent him a text.

I know you're in there, let me in.

After a short pause I received his reply.

Where are you?

I texted my reply

Outside, where do you think?

After another short pause he replied

Hang on a minute

After a few minutes lights came on downstairs and I could hear the door being unlocked. Alex opened the door and stood there in a very short dressing gown. There was a pause as I gazed at his exposed bare legs.

'Don't you feel cold?' I asked.

'Maybe a little,' he replied, 'I think you'd better come in.'

'I thought you'd never ask.'

Alex allowed me past him and re-locked the door.

'What are you doing here this time of night?' He asked.

'I've come to see my favourite physio for a little one to one.'

'Really, I don't remember making an appointment.'

I reached forward and placed my hand through his dressing gown, he was naked underneath.

'I didn't think we needed an appointment for what I have in mind' I said with a wink of the eye.

'I think you'd better come upstairs.'

'I was hoping you'd say that.'

He led me into his apartment which I thought looked tidy for a single man, if not a little Spartan. 'You don't have too much stuff in here, do you? I asked him.

'I've enough' he replied.

Being drunk, I unashamedly answered, 'You have enough for me big boy.'

I pushed myself up against him to see if he was aroused by the fact I had so obviously come for one reason and one reason only. I was disappointed to find that he wasn't. Maybe I had surprised him and he needed a little more encouragement so I unzipped the back of my dress, letting it fall to the floor around my ankles.

'Are you getting ready for bed?' I asked him.

'Well, I was and then some crazy drunk woman started hammering on my door,' he replied.

'Don't let me stop you,' I said as I reached between my back and unfastened the clasp of my bra, easing the straps over my shoulders and throwing it carelessly across the room. I wrapped an arm around his waist and drew us close together again, my other hand searching for the opening in the dressing gown below his waist until I found his growing erection. I wrapped my fingers around the skin of his arousal.

'Oh god Rebecca,' he moaned.

'That's better,' I said. 'I was wondering if you really liked me at all.'

I untied the loose knot of the belt, scarcely keeping the dressing gown shrouding his beautiful body. Alex was panting, unable or unwilling to reply that he liked me but the strength of his erection spoke for him. I was in control and I knew what I wanted so I guided him, pushing him backwards towards the sofa, unsure if it would be long enough for what I had in mind but not caring at that precise moment. We'd improvise. He fell onto the sofa as the back of his legs hit the cushions.

'Oh Rebecca,' he panted again, his vocabulary limited to those few words as he watched me brazenly place my thumbs into the waistband of my panties, pushing them down to reveal all of me to him. I kept my four and a half inch heels on.

'Look at you, you're so magnificent, you're beautiful,' he added.

I wanted to see all of him too; I wanted to see his magnificent body and feel the contours of his chest and the sculpture of his six-pack with my fingertips. I climbed astride his prone body; I noticed him wince as I straddled him. But hardly caring I wanted to see all of him, just as he was seeing all of me and pulled open his dressing gown to reveal the body I yearned for but I didn't expect to be shocked by what I saw.

'Alex, you're hurt,' I gasped as I saw the ugly bruises on his abdomen.

Immediately I scrambled off him.

'What are you stopping for?' Alex gasped.

I knelt on the floor next to him, my fingers oh so gently brushing against the purple and greenish welts. The location of his injuries brought unpleasant memories, memories I thought long forgotten, back into vivid focus.

'Alex, you're injured,' I whispered.

'Oh, that? It's nothing. It was just a small accident in the gym,' he replied pulling his dressing gown around himself, his erection now waning.

I also gathered my dress in front of me to cover my nakedness, feeling suddenly sober and shamefully exposed.

'Nothing… but those bruises look so angry and whatever happened must have been really painful to have caused them, surely?'

'I was doing some bench pressing without a spotter, lifting too much weight and I dropped it. It was my own fault, I should have known better. Don't worry; it looks worse than it really is. It's just the colour of the bruising that's coming out now.'

I looked at his strong arms and wondered how they could have failed him. Had he really been so

142

stupid not to take the precautions that he would have advised others to take? I leant over to kiss his forehead of the man I suddenly had compassion for. I scooped up my clothes, so easily discarded a few moments ago, when I felt a different desire to the one I felt now.

'Don't go Rebecca,' Alex pleaded.

* * *

I woke with a sore head, sunlight breaking through the edges of the drawn curtains. The sound of a boiling kettle and the chinking of crockery told me Alex was up and in the kitchen making a hot drink. I turned over in bed to feel the space where Alex had laid next to me all night. I remembered how we had kissed each other and how we had laid in each other's arms until sleep had taken over. That was last night and this morning my head hurt from the many glasses of Prosecco I had consumed and my feet were sore from the endless dancing in ridiculous heels.

Alex entered the bedroom with a steaming cup of coffee in one hand and a glass of water with two ibuprofen tablets in the other.

'Good morning sleepy head, thought these might help,' he said.

Our lips greeted each other again.

'Your breath isn't the sweetest this morning.' He walked over to the window and drew back the curtains.

'Ah, Alex no,' I groaned, shielding my eyes from the morning sun.

'Someone will be late for work this morning.'

'What time is it?'

'It's just turned eight.'

'Oh no, I've got to open up the gallery.'

I attempted to get out of the bed and swung my legs over the edge of the mattress but when I tried to stand up the room moved and I fell backwards again. Alex lifted my legs back onto the bed and covered me with the duvet.

'I think you need to drink that coffee and take those pills before you think of going anywhere,' Alex advised.

'But it's Saturday and I have to be there to let Lucy into the gallery.' I complained, reasoning with Alex.

Alex plumped up two extra pillows behind me as I half lay, half sat swallowing the tablets he handed me and washing them down with gulps of cold water. 'I can open up for you and I'll wait until you can get there so you don't have to hurry,' He offered.

'You'll need my keys and the alarm code to do that.'

'If you have your keys on you, just tell me what the code is and I'll open up for you. You know you can trust me.'

I told Alex to take the bunch of keys from my handbag and recited the six digit alarm code to him, which he wrote on a scrap of paper.

144

'See you later on, no need to rush. Just come when you're ready,' Alex said as he kissed me on the cheek.

Then he left the apartment, and I heard him walk down the stairs, closing the door to the street behind him and I was left alone in the silence.

CHAPTER 13

Oliver had fulfilled Robins' command to get the alarm code to Rebecca's gallery. Armed with the six digits on the scrap of paper that Alex had given him, he stood outside the gallery door with the key he had copied.

Sunday night is a good time as any to commit a discrete break-in. Streets made quiet by people preparing for a new working week meant that Oliver was unnoticed as Toby barked at him, 'Hurry and get the fucking door open.'

'Shush Toby, not so loud.'

'There's no-one around to hear us. Just get a bloody move on will you?'

Oliver turned the key in the lock and pushed the handle down, opening the door. Immediately the alarm control panel burst into life, its pre-alarm warning bleeping loud enough for Oliver's heart to beat double time and for his hands to shake as he scurried to the control panel. He attempted to hold a torch steady enough to read the numbers on the paper, but Oliver was not cut out to be an art thief and fear, or was it adrenalin, was making his hands shake even more wildly.

Toby closed the door behind them and snatched the paper, on which the safe combination was written, from Oliver's quivering hand.

'Give that here, I'll do it. Make sure the front door is locked you useless prick,' He snarled.

Oliver did as he was ordered and Toby effortlessly quieted the door alarm warning.

Toby took control of opening the safe. Oliver thought the burly man seemed quite expert at the way he spun the safe's lock cylinder one way then the other and wondered how many other safes that didn't belong to him he'd opened?

'Right it's open,' Toby announced as he swung the safe door ajar.

***

Across London, south of the river at Greenwich, Alex waited outside Oliver's apartment building until someone opened the secure entrance door through which he swiftly side-stepped before in closed again. He rode the lift to the fifth floor and Oliver's apartment. Getting a copy of the front door key to get inside had been a simple task. Having watched Oliver copy Rebecca's keys by taking photographs, Alex realised that he didn't have access to the same illegal means of duplication. So when Oliver was distracted, Alex merely picked up his bunch of keys and walked down the street from his studio where the ironmonger cut a copy in two minutes.

Alex knew where Oliver was, he was breaking into Rebecca's gallery, so this gave him ample time to carry out his own small robbery. He also knew what he was looking for, the disc on which the incriminating, yet innocent, video of him treating Mrs. Pearson was recorded.

He stepped inside, closing the door quietly behind him, and was shocked. Alex was astounded to see this expensive home was the most untidy place he had ever seen. Out of date, thick Sunday newspapers and their supplements were strewn about the place. Oliver's clothes dumped just about everywhere. 'How can a person live in this untidy mess?' thought Alex.

Fortunately, Alex's assumption that the disc he sought would not be too hard to find proved true. A stack of DVD's without their boxes sat on top of the player. Sifting through them, Alex found a disc marked *Mother's bedroom* amongst the pile.

Ensuring he had the correct one, Alex slipped the disc into the DVD player and turned on the TV. He watched in silence as images of him conducting physiotherapy treatment to the frail lady played on the screen. He was lost in thought, reminded of how Mrs. Pearson had helped his career. He remembered how kind and generous she had been, then wondered how on earth she could be a mother to that vile, contemptible son of hers, Marcus.

He snapped out of his trance, remembering that he had to get out of the building and be on his way. Alex had found what he came for and slipped the disc into the pocket of his coat. Now he could get out his nightmare and as far away from London as possible. He didn't believe Oliver had any intension of giving him his share of the spoils for robbing Rebecca, and even if he did, he didn't want it now anyway.

Just thirty minutes later Oliver was back in his own flat above the unfinished practice in Putney. Quickly he packed as many belongings as he could into a rucksack, ensuring he had his professional certificates amongst them.

Heading downstairs, Oliver turned off all the lights and opened the door to the street where he was confronted by Robins' two thugs, the ones who had held him to receive the beating from Toby.

'Get your coat on, Mr. Robins wants to see you,' said the Pushy Guy.

'What for? My business with him is done now. He's got what he wanted,' Alex replied and moved to close the door on them.

The Pushy Guy placed one hand on the door to stop it closing and with the other hand opened his jacket to reveal a handgun in a shoulder holster. 'Get your coat on,' he repeated.

***

'Now hurry up and take out what you need.' Toby snarled at Oliver.

Oliver moved forward and breathed a sigh of relief when he recognised the battered flat cardboard box he had hoped was still there. With shaking hands he carefully and almost reverently removed the precious object from the safe.

'This is it Toby, this is what we came for.'

'Don't you think you ought to check that bloody drawing is actually in the box?' Toby suggested sharply.

The broad grin on Oliver's face suddenly disappeared. 'Oh yes, of course,' he agreed.

Laying the box down on Rebecca's desk Oliver cautiously lifted the lid to reveal the Michelangelo drawing covered by a thin transparent, protective sheet.

'That's the one Toby,' Oliver confirmed. 'This is the work of the master himself, only ever seen by a few privileged eyes.'

Toby went to remove the protective film and take a closer look at the artwork his boss was so very keen to get his hands on. Oliver slapped the hand away, for the first time taking control of the situation, as if by gaining the artefact it gave him authority over Toby.

'Don't touch it,' Oliver's newfound confidence in the situation allowed him to say. 'This is a delicate and priceless work of art that's possibly only been touched by very few hands. It doesn't need your fat, sweaty fingers all over it.'

Toby looked suitably chastened by Oliver's reprimand. 'Shut the safe, we're finished here.'

Toby did as commanded, locking the safe and after resetting the alarm system the pair sped away to deliver the valuable package to Mr. Robbins.

***

Alex waited for Oliver and Toby to arrive in the boat that Robins' men had taken him to. Actually, it was more like a ship than a boat, thought Alex, although maybe that was going a little over the top. However, the vessel was stunning. Robbins *Sunseeker* Luxury yacht was maybe a testament to the fact that crime might pay after all.

For the most part Alex had sat in silence in the splendour of the yacht's salon, watched by the men who had made sure he was there. Robins had spent most of the time talking discretely at the far end of the room with a thin, older man wearing unfashionable horn-rimmed spectacles.

Eventually Robins acknowledged Alex's presence.

'How kind of you to join us,' He said sarcastically. 'Hopefully we'll only keep you little while longer if everything has gone to plan. Well done for getting the alarm code to enable our little exercise to take place this evening. How did you do it or am I asking you to reveal trade secrets?'

'Nothing so interesting, I'm afraid, just a lucky break,' replied Alex.

Robins threw his head back and laughed loudly. His two unpleasant employees laughed along with him, unsure why exactly they were doing so, but keen to curry favour with their boss regardless.

'Ha ha, well that was lucky for all of us then wasn't it Alex? Are you absolutely sure you won't stick around? I could really use a resourceful young man like you, especially one with a high I.Q. unlike that of my usual operatives.' He glanced toward his two thugs who stood grinning, unsure of what their boss had just implied but pretty sure it wasn't a compliment.

'Thanks for the offer, but I think I'll be moving on. I haven't found the South of England a particularly friendly place to be honest.' Alex replied also glaring at the pair.

Robins chuckled again. 'Suit yourself Alex, missing gravy on your chips hey?' The southerners all laughed at the cultural stereotype.

'I have to say, you have a fine boat here Mr. Robins. I bet you could sail into any port in the Med and back home again, stuffed with all sort of illegal substances and no one would bat an eyelid?' Alex dared to suggest.

The two thugs made to move forward to punish Alex for his insolence, but Robins' shake of the head told his men that wasn't necessary.

'Oh no Alex, this is my private yacht. I have other people who do that for me. But shall I tell you a little secret? This beautiful craft comes in very useful when I have some artwork to transport. Have you ever heard the phrase, hiding things in plain sight? I can just hang them on the walls of the salon here and nobody is ever the wiser?' Robins smiled at his own cunning. 'Now if you'll excuse me for a few moments.' With that Robins returned to his thin guest at the end of the room.

All Alex wanted was to get off the boat, back to his flat to collect his few belongings and get as far away as possible. He no longer believed that Oliver's promises were anything other than hot air.

He was shocked when he learned of the huge sum of money Robins had vowed to pay Oliver to help steal the drawing in Rebecca's safe and doubted he would ever see a single penny of it himself.

Alex had learned by now that Oliver's greed was such that he would go to any length to prevent himself from giving up any of it. He feared that Oliver might use the threat of going to the police to tell them of his part in Mrs Pearson's suicide to achieve that. But the money Oliver promised him meant nothing to Alex now.

All Alex felt was disgust for himself. He had been part of a terrible, sordid scheme, backed into a corner by Oliver. He realised that he had been only too ready to accept the lies he had spun about Rebecca to justify his initial agreement to the loathsome plot.

Alex hated himself for it, vowing now to leave London altogether, to flee from Rebecca and the betrayal of her trust in him. The only thing he could console himself with was the fact that Rebecca would come to no physical harm. Quite what other sort of harm he had caused her, Alex dreaded to think. He was taking the coward's way out and would run away.

Footsteps sounded on the wooden jetty outside and there was slight movement on the boat in the water as people came on board.

Oliver was once again grinning like the cat that got the cream, only this particular cream was the box he carried proudly in front of him. Toby followed sullenly, ignored in the excitement which Oliver was claiming all for himself.

'Here, as promised is a never seen before preliminary drawing by Michelangelo for his long lost masterpiece, *Leda And The Swan*.'

Oliver proudly placed the thin box on the table before Robins who slid it along to the thin man with the horn-rimmed spectacles.

'Okay Simon, do your thing and verify that this is what I've been waiting to get my hands on for so long.'

Evidently Simon was Robins' own personal art expert and Alex wondered how many other stolen pieces of artwork had been placed before this man.

Oliver stood with his chest puffed up with satisfaction at a job well done and was already spending his newfound wealth in his head. Alex remained seated, unnoticed by the others on-board the boat, waiting for his opportunity to slip away from this band of crooks and leave London altogether, to begin again somewhere else, although he did not understand where or how.

All eyes watched as Simon settled a pair of half-moon reading glasses onto his long, thin nose and pulled a pair of white cotton gloves onto his hands. Carefully he lifted the lid of the box and set it aside, peeled back the translucent paper protecting the contents and with the utmost care lifted out the drawing with his fingertips.

The thin bespectacled face studied the object he held gently, lifting his head slightly to peer through the lens perched on the end of his nose. The room held its breath awaiting his expert affirmation.

'What the hell is this supposed to be?' he asked, raising his gaze to Oliver for an answer.

'It's a priceless work of art for God's sake,' scoffed Oliver. 'Maybe you haven't been privileged to recognise such greatness before?' Oliver attempted a nervous laugh as he looked around at the eyes that were now focussed on him, his precious swagger replaced by nervousness at the expert's brash question.

'I recognise a photograph when I see one, that's for sure. But a photograph of what, who knows? You're wasting my time here.'

Simon took off the white gloves, stowed his reading glasses in his jacket's top pocket and packed away his belongings into his briefcase. He casually flipped the disputed object along the table to Robins.

'I'm done here,' Simon added, as he rose to leave draping his coat over his arm. 'Contact me again Mr. Robins when you have something worth looking at.'

With that he left, leaving the boat in silent tension.

Oliver snatched the item he had conspired so long to steal, out of Robins' hands, feeling the texture of it, turning it over to look at the back in a vain hope that the reverse side would offer some explanation but it didn't.

There was no mistaking what Oliver had in his hands was a photograph. It was on very high quality photographic paper, but a photograph nevertheless.

'Err…err, I don't understand. It was real, I know it was real.'

Robins snatched the object back from Oliver and ran his fat fingers over its surface to prove to himself that what his expert had so curtly revealed was true. 'Have you ever actually seen this so called drawing?'

Oliver was ashen faced, 'Yes, of course I have.' He protested.

'Have you touched it, felt it? Couldn't you tell it was a bloody photograph for god's sake?'

'Yes… no. It's a priceless work of art, it would have been fragile and Rebecca always kept it covered to protect it.'

'To protect it from a fool like you, she's been stringing you along you useless bloody idiot. No wonder her father was so evasive when questioned about it. If it hadn't been for his stupid drunken mouth believing in his own lies to try to impress me, he might be alive today. And to think we were impressed with his apparent courage when the boys here tried to persuade him to hand it to us. The old fool, all he had was a photograph of some old drawing.'

'It's true I tell you,' pleaded Oliver. 'I know it's real. She has it, Rebecca has it.'

'Shut up you clown. Get this pair off my boat,' bellowed a now furious Robins.

Toby didn't need a second invitation and grabbed Oliver by the back of his neck and twisting one of his arms up his back, frog-marched him off the boat.

Alex raised his hands in submission to the other pair of thugs showing he didn't need such rough persuasion to encourage him to get up and move. One of them walked in front of Alex, the one with the gun followed behind with an occasional push in the back to let Alex know he was there. Not that he needed reminding. Robins followed the group, bringing up the rear.

They emerged into the night air onto the jetty where the boat was moored. Alex looked around him to see if any of the other boats had lights burning in their cabins, but the Marina was deserted.

Oliver was by now screaming his innocence, begging to be let go back to the gallery and look in the safe again. No one was listening to him. Instead, Oliver was dragged by Toby and one of Robins' other men to the end of the jetty toward the black open expanse of the marina's water.

Alex stayed next to the boat, the thug with the gun keeping guard over him. Robins strode towards the end of the jetty where Oliver was now crying pitifully.

Alex couldn't help but feel sorrow for the man, even though he had come to despise him. Alex knew Oliver was about to die and he also knew his own life would end if he didn't come up with a plan. But what could he do? There were four of them and one of them was armed with a gun.

Toby forced both Oliver's hands behind his back and tied them together with a thick plastic tie-wrap. Oliver was sobbing uncontrollably, begging, pleading for his life as Robins strode up to him.

'I had a buyer all lined up for a priceless Michelangelo drawing and you've made a fool of me. Nobody makes a fool out of me,' he growled at Oliver, 'nobody!'

'Please Mr. Robins, please, please. I won't tell anyone I promise,' Oliver bawled.

'Shut the big baby up,' Robins ordered his men.

Toby's fist smashed into Oliver's stomach, knocking all the breath from his lungs, forcing him to fall to the deck and gasp painfully for air. Robins' two men then tied a rope around Oliver's ankles, fixing the other end of the rope to a block of concrete.

Alex looked on horrified, recognising how prepared Robins and his men were for this activity. It was clear to him that there was never any chance of getting out of this alive. There was never the half a million pounds Oliver craved for.

Then, with no prompting, the two men pushed a gasping Oliver off the end of the jetty into the dark water.

Alex didn't wait to hear the splash, he didn't wait for his hands to be tied, he didn't wait to be shot in the back. He took off like a rocket as fast as his legs would carry him toward the three men at the end of the jetty who were still looking into the water where Oliver had sunk.

The man with the gun shouted a warning but Alex was banking on him not daring to fire his weapon for fear of hitting his boss.

Within a few bounds Alex dropped his shoulder like a rugby player would and drove it full pelt into Toby's guts, as the thickset turned in reaction to his colleague's warning.

They both hit the water with a crash, following Oliver's body deep down into the cold darkness. Alex had known that he was going under water and had taken lungful's of air into his chest, expanding his lungs to maximum capacity but Toby was caught completely off guard by Alex's shoulder charge. The air was forced from the big man. He kicked to get to the surface to breathe again, but Alex would not let him. He swam behind the floundering, fat man and felt for Toby's jacket in the gloom and when his hands located the collar Alex pulled the jacket down pinning Toby's arms behind him.

The thickset man was in full panic now, just as Oliver had been moments earlier. He wriggled to free himself, but Oliver held him firm. Toby kicked his legs in a desperate attempt to swim upwards but Alex kicked in the opposite direction, keeping them both submerged.

Alex felt his own lungs were about to burst and wondered how long he could hold on to his adversary until he felt Toby's struggle grow weaker until at last he was still.

Alex rose to the surface for air, knowing he was still not safe. He attempted to swim under the wooden jetty where his three opponents stood and as luck would have it, he rose to the surface beneath them. But Alex's gasps for air betrayed his presence.

'He's underneath us,' Alex heard a voice shout.

'Shoot him you idiot,' yelled Robins.

'It might be Toby,' a voice yelled.

'SHOOT,' commanded Robins.

Alex didn't wait to be shot at. He had noticed a large vessel moored at anchor in the middle of the marina's basin and wondered if he could make it that far under water in the dark.

With a final lungful of air he kicked off underwater, hopefully in the boat's direction.

He detected the muffled sound of gunshots and voices shouting, but still Alex kicked on as hard as he could. He was a young, fit and healthy man, athletic and strong, his years of training were now helping to save his life. Even so, Alex wasn't sure if he could make it, his lungs were at bursting point again and just as he was about to rise to the surface for air he felt the underside of the boat brush against his back.

Alex made one last big kick to carry him under the hull and rose at last, gasping for the clear night air.

He was far enough away not to be detected by Robins and his men and he clung to the safety of the boat. Alex could hear Robins' men shouting to recover Toby's body which had floated to the surface.

Alex listened to the distant sounds of the men struggling to pull the dead man's lifeless body from the water. He didn't really know how long he needed to wait behind the safety of his hiding place, but the cold water was making his teeth chatter. Alex looked towards the lights burning at the other side of the marina. It was a long way off and he was getting tired. So he shed the coat he was wearing, which sank to the bottom along with his keys, wallet and the disc he had recovered and using the boat as a shield Alex swam slowly and quietly to the distant bank.

CHAPTER 14

I didn't know whether to laugh or cry. I guess I should be happy for one thing at least. Mum had now recovered from her infection and the angry, disruptive phase she had gone through was over. She was back to normal. But on the other hand I couldn't help but feel sad because what now passed for normal wasn't normal at all. She had changed, our relationship had changed, and I found that just too hard to come to terms with.

I was also very sad that once more a man who I had put my trust in had betrayed me. No, I was wrong; it was worse than sad; I was angry.

I was furious how Alex had turned out to be a wolf in sheep's clothing. How he had callously tried to seduce me. Seduce me into gaining my trust in such a calculated and ruthless way. But maybe I could laugh now after all? Laugh at how I had got the better of him and his accomplice that little shit Oliver.

Mum and I looked at the Michelangelo drawing which I had framed and was now hanging in pride of place in her little room.

Mamma's drawing she called it, remembering how her mother used to show it to her and tell her the story how it had been recused from the retreating German Army as the Americans and British pushed north following the invasion of Italy.

I turned to look at Mum's smiling face; she was so happy, maybe the happiest she had been in a long time. With a joy I had feared she could never express again, she told me all about the drawing.

I smiled along as she described every little detail she has miraculously remembered, despite her illness, so why shouldn't I smile? The ancient drawing was giving her so much joy which was wonderful to see. It didn't really matter to me now how mum could remember things that had happened so long ago and yet almost nothing of recent events. She was in a good place for now at least. What's more, it was fitting that the drawing could now be a blessing to my mother when it had been such a burden to me and my father. A burden which I believe had cost him his life. I also knew who was responsible for that. To me, no longer was my father's death an open verdict. I blamed Mr. Robins for Poppa's murder.

Alex should have been a better liar, instead he told me the truth in that a person can only be hypnotised if they are a willing subject.

I must admit that I was curious to begin with and really taken in by Alex's smooth talk, oh and his skilful hands of course. I willingly submitted myself to him and when I fell into the hypnotic trance for the first time it felt wonderfully real, tranquil, joyous even.

The power of suggestion to my subconscious mind was incredible, but I was also curious to know more of the techniques Alex had used to induce such a powerful trance in me. How had he transported me to places I hadn't physically been to and yet felt so tangible?

163

So, on our last appointment together I decided not to succumb to his velvet voice, but just listen to what he was saying and resist. That was the easy part. I didn't want to fall under his spell so I didn't. The hard part was pretending to be in a dream state without getting angry.

I heard everything. I heard Alex asking me to reveal the safe code to him. I heard Oliver being smart about copying my keys. I heard the quarrel about how they needed my alarm code and how Alex promised to get it out of me.

As I lay on the massage table, my alert, conscious mine was already bent on revenge. And yet there were things that still bothered me about Alex that I couldn't get out my head.

He was always kind and gentle. He always respected my modesty, much to my annoyance at the time. He always covered me over at the end of a session, almost tucking me in like a mother with her child at bedtime. And what about the gentle kiss to my back after our final session?

Robins was a murderous thug, Oliver was a two-faced scumbag, but Alex... what was it about Alex that bothered me so?

Surely I still had every reason to be angry? I was pretty sure now that when he had made love to me for the first time it only a part of his manipulation. Yet hadn't I done the same to him?

The evening I had slipped away from the girl's night out, my plan had been to seduce him in return. With the help of a little Dutch courage I would play the temptress, the femme fatale. Whilst in the throes of passion I would find a way to give him the alarm code he needed, which would lead to his downfall.

Then I saw the bruises on his body and I knew he was lying to me again when he dismissed them as some minor accident. I had wanted the police to arrest him and in that moment I wasn't sure anymore.

Yes, I slept with him, but not in the way I had planned. We didn't make love that night; we just held each other in our arms. And yes, I found a way to give him the code he needed, then when he left me alone in his little flat my plan changed.

A few days earlier I had set to work planning my own strategy for deception. The electrician I had hired wasn't only fixing the lights; he was also installing hidden security cameras. Then a good friend and expert printer made a high quality copy of the drawing which I would use for bait.

Originally I would call the police as soon as I knew they had broken into the gallery. The cameras would provide the evidence needed to identify the culprits and duplicate keys would prove further guilt. But what about Alex, what would happen to him?

I doubted myself and how I would explain everything to the police. Excuse me officer, I allowed a man to hypnotise me so I would reveal secrets about a piece of artwork that may or may not legally belong to me, oh and I've also been having rampant hot sex with him. I don't think so, do you?

Then late Sunday evening my mobile phone alerted me to uninvited guests entering the gallery, and I could even watch Oliver and the fat man who works for Robins go about their evil deed. It relieved me to see Alex wasn't with them.

I'd love to know how long it took them to discover that for all their efforts they were only rewarded with a photograph of a drawing. I wondered how Oliver had tried to explain that away, but what did I care?

This morning the locksmith had called round to the gallery and changed the locks. I had also made sure I changed both the safe combination and the alarm code.

I looked up at the drawing again and couldn't help but think about Alex. Where was he now, I wondered, still in his little apartment above the studio? Probably not, I told myself, he's probably long gone by now.

Nevertheless, I needed to know what it was that bothered me about Alex. I had seen the ugly bruises on his body and I was reminded again of the coroner's report following Poppa's death and the details of similar injuries. I wanted to be angry with him. I wanted to shout at him. 'Tell me your sweet lies,' I longed to yell into his face and see his reaction.

A chill went up my spine. Where was Alex now?

PART 3

CHAPTER 15

I'm a wreck. I'm a mess. My emotions are shot to pieces and I wonder if I'll ever get back to a life that's normal again, or at least something that passes for normal.

I hope today I am making that first step back to normality. I hope the familiar surroundings of the National Gallery will help me do that.

It was only three days after I had hung 'Mamma's drawing' in my mother's room at the nursing home that she passed away peacefully in her sleep. I'd like to think those last three days however were happy ones. Mum spent almost every waking hour staring at the drawing and smiling, so at least it had brought some happiness to the family however briefly. Yet I knew I couldn't keep hold of it, that drawing had already caused too much trouble for us so maybe it was time for me to let go of it and the bad memories that went with it.

Contacting old colleagues at the National seemed to be the logical thing for me to do and when I informed them I had somehow discovered a previously unknown original Michelangelo drawing in the estate of a recently deceased person, I fully expected them to turn up evidence that it previously belonged to a gallery or collection in Italy. But they could find no record of the existence of the drawing. It seemed the mystery of 'Mamma's drawing' deepened.

The National Gallery experts studied the ancient artwork, comparing it to the *After Michelangelo painting of Leda and The Swan* that hangs there. They called other experts from the Queens Collection in to offer their opinion about its authenticity. All the experts agreed that the sketch was an original Michelangelo preliminary drawing for *Leda And The Swan*. The experts also agreed that it was practically priceless, but if they did have to assign a value to it, then the estimate was in the region of the £15 million. Believe it or not, it relieved me I didn't have that significant price tag associated with me any longer.

I wasn't that keen on attending the press conference at the National Gallery but I was assured that my anonymity was secure and anyway the story that the drawing was discovered hanging on the wall of some recently departed old lady was far more newsworthy and it wasn't exactly a lie.

Keeping out of the way was fairly easy. The newspaper photographers were more interested in capturing the money shot, which I thought was ironic, while the BBC correspondent wanted to talk to a big cheese from the National Gallery, or at least someone in a suit who looked like they might know what they were talking about.

There were a lot of familiar faces in the gathering and one or two of them were gracious enough to come over to express their condolences over mum's passing. I kept the conversation short, which I think suited everyone.

Then across the room I noticed someone who I didn't want to talk to. I got the feeling that he had been watching me for some time and when I made eye contact with him he made a beeline for me. He wasn't someone I particularly wanted to talk to, but I would not show I feared him and run away.

'Hello Rebecca, how good to see you again,' Robins said to me.

I just stood there and didn't respond to his false greeting but one thing was for sure, it was not good to see him. I considered turning my back on him and walking away, but I waited for Robins to tell me why he had walked over to speak to me. He hadn't come over to say hello or for some nice friendly chat because we were so not friends.

'Isn't it wonderful that they have unearthed this valuable work of art after all this time? I had heard rumours about its existence but I never thought for a moment it was true. You know Rebecca, there are so many dishonest people around in the art world and they give the business a bad name.' Robins gestured to the Michelangelo drawing on display and took a step closer to me. 'Some dishonest person might even try to copy such a masterpiece and pass it off as an original.'

I considered not responding to his taunts but my blood was boiling now and maybe it was adrenaline or maybe stupidity but I matched his step forward to me with one of my own so we stood face to face just inches apart.

'And some dishonest bastard might even try to steal such a masterpiece. They might even murder for it.'

I couldn't believe those words came out of my mouth. For a brief moment it horrified me that I had dared to say such things to this man, given his reputation, but the strangest thing happened. Robins looked genuinely shocked at my apparent bravery and he retreated a couple of paces.

'Err... I, suppose it was your mother's estate this piece came from? I'm sorry for your loss.'

'You don't know sorry and you don't get to talk about my mother.' I was on a roll now.

Robins turned to walk away from me. Maybe he wasn't so tough after all? Then he stopped and turned back to face me, his composure regained.

'By the way, if you see Alex again soon please tell him I'm looking for him.' With that he walked off through the crowd of people and disappeared from view.

I walked over to the long table at the side of the room where glasses of wine and juice were on offer. I selected a glass of white wine and downed it in one go. I picked up a second glass and moved away with the waiting staff staring at me open-mouthed.

I wondered aimlessly around the room, sipping at my second glass of wine, avoiding eye contact with anyone, lost in my own thoughts. Why would Robins mention Alex? Had they not been in the game of deception together? Then I remembered the bruises on Alex's body again.

My hands shaking and in danger of spilling the wine, I retreated into the ladies toilets and set my glass down on the row of washbasins. Leaning forward toward the long mirror above the basins, I stared long and hard at my refection. Then burst into tears.

A woman emerged from one of the cubicles and washed her hands as quickly as she could to escape my blubbing. Dabbing my eyes with a tissue recovered from my handbag, I straightened myself up and gained my composure. Why did I get the feeling that this saga was far from over?

***

The taxi dropped me off outside the shop front where Alex had his studio. I wasn't sure why I was there or what I find, but I would felt I had to try to make some sense of everything that had happened. Alex had lied to me, or at least he had tried to and that was a feeling I knew well. But I was sure that there had been moments of real tenderness between us.

As the taxi pulled away, I glanced across the street and noticed a homeless man camped in the doorway of a vacant shop. There seemed to be so many of these guys on the streets these days and I wondered how society had come to this. As I looked over at him two men in identical, ill-fitting dark suits came out from an adjacent shop where they appear to have purchased pre-packed sandwiches. One of the men had already opened his packet and extracted one of the sandwich triangles. As he walked past the homeless guy he offered the remaining half still in its wrapper and as the homeless guy reached up to accept it, the man quickly withdrew it and instead swung a leg out to kick the poor, unfortunate fellow who curled up in self-protection.

'Hey, you… stop that' I called out, and looked to see if it was safe for me to cross the road.

A stream of cars stopped me going over to check on him and before the flow of traffic stopped the homeless guy gathered his eager belongings and hurried away, head bowed. 'Are you okay?' I shouted after him, but the homeless guy didn't stop to answer me. I turned my attention to the suited men. 'What do you think you're doing?'

Maybe that was probably a reckless thing to do, but instead of shouting back at me the pair hurried to a large red 4x4 and drove off.

I returned to the business in hand and pushed on the door of the shop which to my surprise swung opened. My heart beat fast within my chest, Alex was home. I wasn't sure why I had gone there in the first place and now I was torn between anger and relief. Anger at how he had deceived me but relief that he hadn't disappeared from the face of the earth and somehow wasn't involved with Robins, or at least I prayed that he wasn't.

'Hello, is anybody there?' I called out. The door behind closed behind me and there was an eerie silence inside the reception area of Alex's practice. Everything appeared the same was before, even down to the unfinished building work.

'Hi, it's only me Rebecca,' I yelled. I held my breath as I heard footsteps from the rooms at the back of the building. They grew louder until I saw the handle turn on the door which led to Alex's office. I could hear my heart pounding in my ears as the door opened.

'Alex?'

'No Raj,' said the man who emerged from the door. 'Can I help you? This place isn't open anymore.'

'Oh, I was looking for Alex the Physiotherapist.'

'Yes, so am I, along with the guy that rents my shop.'

'Oliver Crosby?' I asked as my breathing and heartbeat returned to normal.

'Yes, that's him,' replied Raj. 'When I say he rents the place off me, it would be nice to receive some rent. I've not received a penny since they moved in and now it looks as though they've done a runner.'

So the pair of them have disappeared and made themselves scarce, I thought. 'Oh dear, I'm sorry to hear that and the guy who worked here was such a good physio. I don't suppose I'll be able to finish my treatment now then?'

'Sorry miss, I'm afraid not.'

'It's just that I think I left my coat here last time I had an appointment.'

'Take a look around and see if you can find it,' invited the shop owner. 'I'm salvaging anything they've left behind that's worth selling, but there isn't much to be honest and look at what they've done in this room. Started some renovations and just left it half done. I'll have to spend more money myself to let it out again. That Oliver bloke seemed an honest sort, and he was so well spoken I thought he would be the trustworthy type.'

'You never can tell,' I replied. 'A posh accent can hide a multitude of sins.'

'Hmm, I just hope he gets what he deserves.'

'Absolutely,' I agreed

Having been given permission to roam around I stepped through into the back rooms followed by Raj. He had the door to the treatment room open and appeared to be packing anything that may be worth salvaging into boxes. I looked around the room that Alex had used as his office and noticed that his certificates were missing from the wall.

'Do you mind if I look upstairs?' I asked Raj. 'He may have taken it up there for safekeeping.'

'Help yourself,' Raj replied boxing up the items in the treatment room.

I climbed the stairs and entered Alex's flat, recalling the events that took place between us the last time I was there. It was still as Spartan as it was before but maybe even more so if that was at all possible. It looked like there was even less in the apartment than there had been when I had taken it upon myself to have a good snoop around when he had left me all alone in there.

Thinking about that now made me feel so terribly guilty. I had looked in all of his drawers and opened all of his cupboards without knowing what I was looking for. Maybe I was hoping to find something to convince me that somehow Alex had been coerced into the plot to rob me? Of course I found nothing then and I could find nothing to help me now either. There was no reason for me to return here, what had I been thinking?

At the bottom of the stairs I thanked Raj for allowing me to look round and with a sigh of resignation, realised this story was now at an end.

I was just about to leave when I noticed a rucksack leaning against the wall by the door. I unzipped the top of the bag and could see it was packed full of clothes... men's clothes.

Did this bag belong to Alex and if so why had he left it here? Apparently Alex had decided to leave, but something or someone must have prevented him from taking the bag with him. This was a new mystery.

I picked up the rucksack, slung it over my shoulder and left for home.

The homeless guy watched Rebecca leave with the rucksack.

CHAPTER 16

Once back at my apartment I threw the rucksack on my bed and opened it up. If the rucksack had stood by the door since the night of the attempted robbery at the gallery, Alex hadn't returned for it. Could it be that he was in no position to return for it? The thought of what might have happened to him frightened me. I tried to think positive and remembered that Robins had suggested that he didn't know Alex's whereabouts when he asked if I had seen him.

I looked at the contents of the bag. Nestled between the clothes were his degree and Society of Physiotherapy certificates. So that said to me Alex was planning to move on, perhaps start a new life somewhere else. What had stopped him I wondered and would he return to his little flat to collect this bag at some point? Was he even able to return to the flat?

One thing he could do however was pack a bag well. Everything was neatly folded and packed with every potential hole filled with rolled up socks or a Tee-Shirt. It was better than I could ever manage.

When I pack a case, it always ends up resembling a small mountain of clothes, thrown in haphazardly, no matter how hard I try. Then closing it usually requires sitting on the case and with the help of at least one other person to squash it shut. If I'm ever asked to open it at customs, I worry that all my garments will burst out like a jack-in-the-box. I also noticed that Alex had only packed two pairs of shoes. I couldn't cope on a long weekend with only two pairs of shoes.

Sitting on the bed next to Alex's clothes, I picked up a well-folded shirt and held it to my face to see if it smelled of him. But the only scent I could smell was that of laundry. It seemed all traces of him were gone. Where was he?

Even though I had vowed to myself, I would never ever do it, I phoned Oliver's mobile. I would ask him only one question. Do you know where Alex is? I wouldn't get into conversation with him, I wouldn't mention that I knew he had tried to rob me, I would only need the answer to that one question… nothing else. But his phone just went straight to voicemail. No doubt he was keeping a low profile. I had run out of ideas and anyway why was I so bothered about this? Alex was a villain, a liar, a cheat, and I wanted nothing more to do with him.

I was brought back to reality when my doorbell rang. I peeped through my door's security spy viewer and was perplexed to see a strange figure outside in the hallway. He was scruffily dressed with a dirty knitted hat pulled down over his ears. He sported a straggly beard and although I couldn't get a look at his face as he was nervously looking back and forth along the corridor outside my door I vaguely recognised him as the homeless guy I had seen opposite Alex's practice earlier.

179

What was he doing here, had he followed me home? I stepped away from my door, afraid of what to do. Should I call the Concierge and ask him to come up to deal with him? The doorbell rang again, making sure the security chain was in place and with great care I slowly opened the door a little to the extent the chain would allow.

'Who are you? What do you want here,' I said nervously.

'Rebecca, it's me. It's Alex.'

For a moment I was shocked, speechless, I stood open-mouthed unable to move. I slammed the door shut and just stood there looking at it. There was a gentle knock and the voice on the other side said in half a whisper.

'Rebecca it's me let me in… please?'

Taking a deep breath, I gathered myself together, took the security chain off, opened the door wide, grabbed the vagrant his lapels, dragged him inside, kicked the door shut and pulled his face to meet mine to kiss him hard on his mouth.

'My God you stink,' I shrieked, recoiling at his disgusting state.

'I know, sorry.'

I stood back to get a good look at him, studying his strange, dishevelled condition, then straightened the palm of my right hand and slapped him hard across the cheek. The sound of the slap was as sharp and as crisp as they sound in the movies. Rather pleasing, I thought.

'I guess I deserved that,' said Alex after he had recovered from the unexpected blow.

He deserved more than that, I thought, after everything he's done, clenching my right hand into a fist.

The punch I landed on his face really hurt like hell. I don't know what Alex's face felt like, but my hand was in agony. This was definitely not like the movies; it felt like I had broken every bone in my hand. My fingers throbbed, and I shook them out to try to alleviate the throbbing.

'God Rebecca, I think you've broken my nose,' moaned Alex, his hand to his face.

'Good. You deserve it, you bastard,' I replied shaking my fingers and rubbing them with my other hand.

Alex touched his face to assess the damage. He didn't have a bloody nose, but I had split his lip, of which I was quite proud. He touched his injured lip and noticed there was blood and then for some unknown reason we began to laugh. Giggling to begin with until we were roaring with laughter, huge belly laughs until our sides hurt.

Eventually our laughter died down, and we stood in the silence, staring at each other.

'I'm so sorry Rebecca,' Alex said.

'Me too,' I answered.

***

In the silence of my sitting room Alex told me all about his desire to be the best physiotherapist he could. He told me about Mrs. Pearson, about Marcus and the blackmail. How he had been befriended and lied to by Oliver. He told me the whole sordid story and as I listened, I allowed him to off-load his burden of guilt and shame. My heart went out to him.

'On our last massage session in your treatment room, I wasn't under hypnosis Alex. I was pretending, so I heard everything you were trying to do,' I confided.

'Ah, I didn't know that.'

'I know you didn't, I'm an extremely good actor. I also heard Oliver and you arguing so I prayed that there was a chance you weren't one hundred percent involved. I appreciate you telling me everything, and I think I can understand how trapped you were. I can't believe I let myself be taken in by him. It's my own fault for confiding in him I guess.'

I heard myself say the words and instantly felt angry that I was letting him off the hook so easily, but then again I had drawn blood so maybe I'd given him enough of a hard time. But the truth was, I wanted so badly to believe him… to forgive him despite everything. It was Oliver I was really mad with now. How I'd love to smack him on the nose right now.

'Don't blame yourself. Nothing about this whole thing was ever your fault,' Alex assured me.

'Except for that damned drawing, I wish I had got rid of it sooner. But tell me,' I asked Alex. 'Did you really believe that you could hypnotise me into giving away all of my secrets?'

For the first time since Alex had told me his story, he allowed himself a little smile. 'To be honest, I wasn't sure,' he admitted. 'I think it would have needed more time and more sessions added to your gift certificate.'

We both smiled at that. Secretly, I was amazed at how cunning Oliver had become to get what he wanted. Maybe people with obsessions become the most inventive? I allowed Alex to continue.

'Hypnosis is supposed create a level of consciousness where a person becomes highly responsive to suggestions. Of course the suggestions have to be believable and used correctly they allow modification to that person's behaviour. I tried to paint a picture in your mind that you would believe. I had no idea if it would work, but what choice did I have?'

'The first time you hypnotised me it worked,' I admitted. 'Maybe we'll never know if I would have genuinely given you the safe combination for real?'

'The whole charade exhausted me,' said Alex. 'All the of the scheming, the lying, all of that for a fake.'

I settled back into my seat. Of course, I hadn't told him the whole story. 'I switched them when I figured out you were trying to learn my safe code and that Oliver was behind it. I knew it was the Michelangelo drawing he was after. He'd become obsessed by it. So I had a friend, a very talented friend, make a copy for me and I switched them. Oliver stole a copy.'

'A copy... poor Oliver,' said Alex, his face downcast.

I was outraged.

183

'Don't give me poor Oliver. I leant him money for his stupid get rich schemes, confided in him, I've been let down by him and then he tries to steal from me. And I'm supposed to feel sorry for him.'

'Oliver's dead Rebecca.'

'What… how? How is he dead?'

'When Robins found out the drawing wasn't real, he had his men beat him really badly. Then they tied him up and threw him in the Thames with a weight around his ankles.'

'Oh my god no… it's all my fault he's dead. Why didn't I just call the Police and tell them that a break-in was in progress? I never wanted that to happen'

I sobbed uncontrollably. By being so smart a man was dead. Oh, the fear and terror he must have felt and all because of me. The poor man, he may have turned bad but before that he was my friend; did I really want him to be murdered in such a terrible way?

Alex came over and sat on the arm of the chair next to me. He placed his arm around my shoulders and kissed me gently on my forehead.

'No Rebecca, it's not your fault at all. Robins planned all along to get rid of us both. He had everything prepared to make sure we were out of the way permanently. I would be dead too if I hadn't made a last-minute break for freedom. As it is, I had to take someone's life to escape. Remember that fat guy that Robins bought to the gallery? The one I had a tussle with? I drowned him and it was awful but I had to, it was him or me.'

Tears streamed down my face. In trying to be smart two men were now dead because of me. There was no longer any love lost between Oliver and me, but he'd died. Murdered in the most violent and terrible way. Nobody deserved that, not even Oliver. My scheming was responsible for his death.

Alex knew my thoughts, it seemed.

'Listen Rebecca, you cannot and must not blame yourself. Oliver was no saint, he knew the sort of people he was mixed up with and to be honest neither you nor I know what else he was involved in. People that live by the sword hey?'

'You're probably right Alex,' I conceded, mildly unconvinced and went to rest my head against his chest. 'Wow Alex, you reek man! Where have you been?' I pulled away from him.

'I've been living by my wits and on the streets. I wanted to see if I could get back to my flat to collect my stuff, but the place was being watched.'

'Watched by who?'

'Robins' men, I knew they'd be looking for me. Remember those two guys in the red car, you know, the ones that tried to kick me? For a moment I thought they might recognise me, but you scared them off.'

'Yes I did, didn't I? Scary that's me.'

Alex touched his split lip. 'Yes remind me never to mess with you again.'

I managed a little chuckle. 'Anyway, don't worry anyway Alex, I have your rucksack, it's in my bedroom.'

'You are an incredibly resourceful woman. Has anyone ever told you that?'

'No, not nearly as often as I would like. Now up with you and get those disgusting clothes off. You need a hot shower and a shave. Don't even think of bringing that horrible hairy face near me until you have.'

'Did you pick up my other bag with my toiletries and shaving kit in them?' Alex asked cheekily.

'Don't push it; you're lucky I didn't give your clothes away to the homeless. They'd be more deserving. You can use one of my Gillette Venus razors for a shave.'

'I can't use a woman's razor,' he complained.

'Why can't you?' I answered. 'They're probably exactly the same except that women pay more. Don't worry, I won't tell anyone. Now go make yourself attractive to me.'

Whilst Alex was in the bathroom I bundled up the dirty clothes he had arrived in and stuffed them in black refuse sacks. The contents of his rucksack I spread over my bed, selected him some things to wear and created some space for his other clothes in the wardrobe and chest of drawers, putting everything away neatly for him.

I did the same around the bed, clearing a shelf by the bedside tables for him and smoothing the duvet down after I had retrieved my pyjamas from under my pillow, then throwing them in the laundry basket. 'Won't need those tonight,' I thought.

The en-suite bathroom door was slightly ajar, and I tip-toed over to take a peek. Alex was standing in front of the mirror finishing shaving his face with my Gillette Venus, a towel wrapped around his waist. Entering the steam-filled room, I walked towards him, wrapping my arms around him and nestled my cheek on his back as he continued his shave.

'The bruises on your stomach, they are Robins doing aren't they?' I asked.

'Uh-huh,' retorted Alex. 'Yes, I'm afraid so, how did you know?'

'Let's call it woman's intuition, never you mind about that, the main thing is that you're alive and not dead. I don't know what I would do if Robins had killed you too. It doesn't bear thinking about.'

With relief and anger, tears of exasperated joy rolled down my cheek. Alex paused, turned to face me and stared directly into my eyes for a minute. He wiped my tears gently with his free hand and placing the razor down pulled me close towards him with both arms whilst placing a long breathless kiss on my lips. I rewarded him with a forceful, desperate kiss of my own. So forceful that I made him wince at his broken lip which I'd given.

Alex wiped his cut lip. A trace of blood remained there and as his mouth met mine, the metallic taste of his blood tingled the tip of my tongue. Face to face we stood now staring into one another's eyes.

187

'Don't move,' I instructed him, as I caressed the back of his head with my hand. My fingers drifted purposely, up and around, caressing his head and hair, like I was discovering him for the first time.

Cautiously Alex responded by moving his hand behind my neck and slowly moving them around my shoulders and down my spine, as though he was offering me his slowest, most passionate massage.

I quickly pulled him close to me so that his torso was touching mine now as we faced one another, lingering to read each other's desire. It was like a slow motion dance and for a fleeting moment I remembered his betrayal, but he was here now, he had come back to me. Should I, could I allow myself to love this man?

I released one of my hands from his hair and let it drop to the towel around his waist. With a tug it was free, and I gasped as I felt him already erect.

His hands move to unbutton my blouse and I assisted him to speed up the process frantically unzipping my skirt to let it fall around my ankles.

He reached behind me to undo my bra and couldn't do it. We both giggled a little like nervous first timers. Hurriedly I helped him unfasten the clasp and as the bra dropped to the floor to join the skirt, my nipples sprang to attention. I want him to touch them and as if he can read my mind he does just that, squeezing them just enough to send shivers right through me.

I'm standing before him in just my shoes and panties and without apology I hurriedly dispose of them so I was as naked as him.

He held me away from him to look at me and I in turn look at his body. I run my hands across his chest, feeling his broad chest and ripped muscles. He is magnificent.

Suddenly, without warning, he swept me up into his arms and carried me toward the shower cubical he has just come from.

'In here?' he asks, as if he needed my permission.

'Oh yes,' I whisper.

I have free hands to turn on the water and the jets burst over us, wetting us all over.

As the jets shower over our bodies he kisses me again, harder this time and I know I want him now, like I have never wanted a man before.

As we stand in the cascading water, his hands explore my body as my hands do his. I take him in my hand and feel the length and width of him.

'Slowly,' he says, as if I am moving too quickly. So I obey, touching him slowly, gently.

Alex manoeuvred me towards the corner of the cubicle where there is a ledge built into the tiling and coaxing my legs apart, I feel breathless as he enters me.

His tongue makes exquisite circles around my nipples, reading my mind like a book. I was in ecstasy, giving myself entirely for his pleasure. Never before had any man made love to me so utterly and completely like this man did now.

The water, his caresses and touches becoming almost too much for me and as his exquisite rhythm begins to increase from slow deliberate lengths of pleasure into hard thrusts against my special place, he fills me completely and then he explodes in sweet agony. With perfect timing I do the same whilst he is still inside me.

My fingers dig deep into his back and I can't help cry out his name.

'Alex!'

'Oh Rebecca,' he moaned in reply.

CHAPTER 17

When I awoke I was warm and secure, nestled in the curve of my lover's body like two spoons lying together in a drawer. The last time I had shared a bed with this man I was dreaming of a way to stop him changing my future; but now it was all so different. As hard as I tried, I couldn't see what any future looked like for us.

His arm wrapped around me I reached for his hand and bought it to my lips to kiss it gently, taking care not to wake him although he was already stirring. I turned over to face him brushing his soft shaven cheek with the back of my hand. We whispered good morning to each other and kissed softly, our eyes closed in the safety of the bed.

We lay next to each other, face to face with no words between us for what seemed like an eternity yet each of us knowing what the other was thinking. I spoke for us both.

'We can't stay this way.'

He wrapped me tightly in his arms so I was almost unable to move. 'Yes we can. Let's stay here all day,' whispered Alex

'You know what I mean.' I replied

Alex released his grip and rolled over onto his back. 'I know.'

As he lay with his hands behind his head I shifted to lie across him.

'Of course I could keep you prisoner in my bed so you'd have to satisfy my wild desires on a daily basis, maybe twice daily.'

'You'll wear me out women, death by sex.'

'What a way to go.' I replied as my cheek lay against his chest.

There was a long silence again until at last Alex spoke again. 'They'll find me eventually if I stay here Rebecca and I won't risk any harm coming to you because of me. My best chance is to get as far away from here as possible.'

'No... no perhaps it isn't,' I exclaimed boldly, throwing the bedclothes from off us exposing our naked bodies to the morning light. 'Come on, get up lazy bones.'

***

We sat at my kitchen table, coffee alerting our senses to the job in hand.

'You witnessed Robins order his men to murder Oliver and you know where to find the body. I'm pretty sure the same people also murdered my father. Now I can't prove that but maybe we can prove he murdered Oliver. We should call the police, you give a statement and Robins gets arrested.'

'You think it's that simple?' Asked Alex

'Yes I do. This is our chance to get even and get him locked away for what he's done. What he did to my poppa.'

'Do you really think I'd survive long as the only witness? I'm pretty sure Robins would see to that.'

'So the Police take you into protective custody.'

'And you? They get to me through you.'

'I can look after myself.'

'You can't Rebecca. They kill people, remember? I won't do it. I'll just pack up my stuff and get out of your life. It'll be safer for us both that way.'

We sat in silence, staring at our coffee cups. I wasn't going to give in so easily. I wanted justice for Poppa and some sort of justice for Oliver. He's got himself involved in this but I still harboured nagging feelings of guilt that I could have prevented his murder. I was resolved to do something to make amends.

'Oliver was never the most honest of men, that much is clear now. If he was involved with Robins in one crooked scheme then he's likely to have been involved in others.'

'I guess that much is true,' Alex agreed.

'So there must be some sort of evidence, something we can find in his apartment right?'

'Maybe, I guess you're right. He did seem to know Robins pretty well, for all the good it did him.'

'Okay so I'm going round his apartment to see if I can find something.'

Alex looked unconvinced and sat back in his chair, arms folded.

'For what purpose, so you find something that links Oliver to Robins and then what?' He asked

'I don't know but it's better than running away and doing nothing.'

'Is it?'

'Yes it is and I've still got a key to Oliver's flat.'

Alex stood up from the table as though he was going to make some sort of dramatic announcement, which of course being a man he did. 'Then I'll go to Oliver's apartment to see if I can find anything that might help us.'

'Oh sit down you big drama queen, you're not going anywhere,' I told him. 'You know Robins' men are looking for you. I'll be perfectly fine, you can stay here and tidy up the place now you're my house slave.'

Alex looked a little crestfallen at my little joke but I found the idea of him being my house slave suddenly appealing.

***

I took the tube over to Oliver's flat as Alex's situation had unnerved me. I somehow felt safer amongst a crowd of people. But exiting the station to walk to where the building was I felt oddly exposed and kept glancing behind me as I walked briskly to the apparent safety of being inside.

I wasn't really sure what I was looking for but Alex's situation had got me spooked. Arriving at the entrance door to Oliver's building I offered the access fob to the reader and the magnetic latches clicked their release and I entered,

194

closing the glass door behind me. I nervously checked that no one was watching me from the outside. Thankfully there wasn't. I took the lift which deposited me on the floor where Oliver's apartment was situated. It was silent as I walked the length of the corridor, the plush carpet under foot ensuring my presence was unannounced. I had always wondered how Oliver managed to afford to live in such a prestigious address, maybe I was about to find out as I placed the key in the lock and stepped inside.

I had only been to this flat once before, that was the week he had moved in and he wanted to impress me. Oliver had presented me with my own set of keys as he proudly showed off his latest new possession.

'Poor Oliver,' I thought. 'He was forever chasing dreams that were out of reach.'

For an expensive luxury apartment the place was remarkably untidy. There were old newspapers on the coffee table and the sofa, clothes thrown over backs of chairs and a pile of dirty crockery piled up in the sink of an open-plan kitchen.

Alex's meagre surroundings had been tidy and clean in comparison which clearly illustrated the character of each man. Where to start looking was the question? The place was a mess and I had no idea what I was actually looking for.

The fact that the place was such a mess didn't help either. Remembering Oliver had used one of the bedrooms as his office it seemed prudent to leave the disarray of his living for his working space. It was no surprise to see the so called office was also a scene of complete chaos. How could Oliver have ever managed to work in these conditions and manage his business interests efficiently? I sat in his office chair and surveyed the jumble of paper and files in front of me, leafing through invoices, receipts and emails he had printed off in hard-copy but none of it of any potential interest.

How had it come to this I wondered? A man with a privileged background, every advantage in life and an excellent education had fallen so badly. I found my answer as I opened the drawers to his desk. Sitting inside were six little plastic bags each containing a white powder. Now I may have led a relatively sheltered life but I'm pretty sure I knew what the powder was. Had Oliver become an addict and needed money to pay a dealer or drug related debts? Had he become a dealer in cocaine himself and got mixed up in some seedy underworld criminal gang?

I considered taking the find with me back to the flat to show Alex, but dismissed the idea as too risky to carry around. I took a photograph of the contents of the draw with my mobile instead.

In the draw below I spotted a laptop, so clearing a space on the cluttered desk I set it down, opened it up and turned it on. The screen lit up to prompt me for a password. Oh, now I was stuck, I had absolutely no idea what the password could be. I tried a series of names, his name, my name, our birthdays. I even tried entering *password* and the numbers 1 to 9.

It was clear that any idea I had of finding anything linking Oliver to Robins was too much to hope for. So spotting a leather briefcase resting against the desk, I bundled the laptop inside and made my way towards the door to leave. Being in a dead man's flat was making me feel uneasy.

CHAPTER 18

I wasn't sure I had returned home with anything of value from Oliver's apartment. What was I supposed to do with a laptop I couldn't access and a photo of what I believed was probably cocaine? My discoveries only served to confirm that the poor man had got mixed up in a world for which he was ill-equipped for. Perhaps, therefore, my mind was not focussed on our situation and I was open to suggestibility, Alex had a way to seemingly influence suggestibility of course and once again I found myself vulnerable to his wiles.

I called out to Alex when I stepped into my apartment as I couldn't see him in the living room. Perhaps he was still in bed I mused, but no it was better than that. He replied to my call with a shout from the bathroom.

'In here', he called back.

Not wanting to miss out on another invitation to join him for activities in the bathroom I poked my head around the half open door to see what he was summoning me to, where I discovered him clearing the shower cubicle, the scene of our most recent encounter, which was now pristine and gleaming. Likewise the mirror, which Alex had polished to within an inch of its life, the sink was clean and more impressively he had actually cleaned the toilet as well. I couldn't believe it?

I felt somewhat faint and stumbled into the living room, noticing how tidy it was with the furniture tidy and cushions plumped up and neatly positioned. All of the crockery from breakfast had been washed and put away.

Alex followed me into the living room, his sleeves rolled up and the cleaning caddy in his hand. Is it me, am I so unusual that the sight of a gorgeous man with his sleeves rolled up performing domestic chores had me feeling incredibly aroused? The stirrings in my nether regions almost caused me to forget the importance of my mission.

'Are you okay?' Alex asked me.

'I'm feeling slightly overwhelmed' I replied truthfully.

Alex placed the cleaning materials on the kitchen counter top.

'Come and sit down for a minute,' he said. 'This is probably all too much for you. It's not the sort of thing that happens every day.'

'You can say that again' I muttered quietly. His still wet hands stoking my desire further. I gathered my strength and clearing my throat decided it was more grown up and decidedly more appropriate to focus on the matter in hand.

'I'm not sure I found anything that might help us' I explained to Alex, once I had regained my composure. 'But it was difficult to actually find anything at all. The place was such a mess it was impossible to know where to start let alone know what I was searching for. It almost looked like the place had been burgled.'

'I remember' agreed Alex 'If it wasn't for the fact that I thought Oliver was likely to have the

199

disc I was looking for as one of his favourites and right next to his TV I'm not sure I would have found it. It was more like a pigsty then a luxury apartment. I don't know how anyone could live like that.'

Then Alex realised what he had said and that Oliver was no longer living at all.

There was a little silence as we remembered the events Alex has described to me. I could see sadness in his eyes, not that there was any love lost between them of course, but to witness such a violent murder, how could any normal person not be affected?

I also thought about the happy young man I had met at university and the person who had shown me such compassion when Poppa had died. How could he have met his end in such a dreadful way? What had led him to go so wrong I wondered?

Opening my handbag I retrieved my mobile phone to select the most recent photograph I had taken inside Oliver's apartment and showed Alex my discovery. 'So I'm thinking this isn't Coffee-Mate' I said, refereeing to the bags of white powder I had taken I had found.

Alex reached out to take the phone from my hand and studied the screen briefly. 'No I don't suppose it is. I'll bet that this lot cost a pretty penny. Maybe from one of Robins' other business enterprises, he hinted as much to me. I'd guess that's how Oliver got to be associated with him in the first place. Got into debt and needed a way to pay off. But maybe we'll never know.'

'No I suppose we never will, but I'm not sure where we go from here.'

'I told you Rebecca, you won't be safe whilst I'm still around. The best thing is for me to get as far away from here as possible.'

I lifted the briefcase I had bought back with me onto my lap. 'You give in too easily, I've got Oliver's laptop here and if we can figure out his password I'm sure we can discover something incriminating.'

I slid the laptop from the case and as I did so a large photograph slid out and floated to the floor. Alex reached down to pick it up. He flipped it over to look at the picture printed on it.'

'I've seen this picture before' said Alex

'What picture?' I queried and took the photograph from him. I studied it for a few minutes and then a slow realisation awakened a vague memory from deep inside me 'So have I' I agreed, suddenly excited. 'This is the picture Oliver tried to show me that day he turned up in the gallery. You remember, the day you were trying to acquire my alarm code? He wandered in with the lame excuse of asking if I was interested in it.'

'I don't mean this photograph, I mean the actual painting' explained Alex.

'You know where it is?'

'Yes… why?'

'Because it's a stolen artwork, or at least I think it is. I can't be sure because this isn't really my area of expertise but I have a vague recollection of its theft, it was in all of the trade press at the time. But why would a stolen painting be hanging on a wall at Mrs Pearson's house?'

'It was her dick-head son Marcus. He started changing things around the house while she was still in it, he just couldn't wait to get his hands on the place. Between you and me, I think he was acting as though his mother was already dead. He really is a little shit. His mother really hated that painting too.'

This was a little confusing to say the least. If Oliver was acquainted with Marcus Pearson and Marcus Pearson had the actual painting why was Oliver trying to offload it to me? 'Do you think Oliver was trying to implicate me in some way? I didn't realise he hated me that much,' I asked Alex.

'Don't give him too much credit for being that devious,' Alex said reassuringly. 'The truth is probably far simpler. We've both seen the state of his flat and I'd put money on that being the first thing he could find. He was really only interested in checking up on me that day. He went nuts when I didn't get to see you setting the alarm; he was terrified of what Robins might do if we didn't get what he wanted.'

Alex' explanation made sense or at least I hoped it did. I couldn't bear the thought of Oliver planning even more misfortune for me. 'That makes more sense I suppose and he knew that Abstract Art isn't my area of interest, but if I am right about this painting and it is stolen I wonder if that could give us some sort of link between Robins and him?'

The perplexed expression on Alex face suggested he wasn't convinced. 'I don't see how,' he said. 'I know where the painting is and I know where Oliver's body is. Do I go to the police and try to tell them what I know? Pearson will claim I murdered his mother and Robins will implicate me in Toby's death. He wouldn't be wrong there either, I did kill him.'

Now it was my turn to settle Alex's nerves, I could see he was beginning to doubt that he could never be free from the dilemma he faced. 'Do you trust me Alex?'

He titled his head sideways and regarded me quizzically. 'What do you mean?'

'I'm asking you seriously Alex. Do you trust me? Not in the way you tried to get me to trust you, do you really trust me?'

Alex folded his hands in his lap and looked down at the floor like a scolded puppy. 'Yes, I trust you Rebecca.'

'Good. Then we have work to do. First, we need to confirm that this is indeed what I think it is, stolen. I know someone who can help me with this and she owes me a favour...a big one.'

Alex lost the puppy dog look and changed his expression to one of quiet concern. 'Why do I get the impression, that you are planning something not quite kosher?'

'What me? Do something inappropriate? That wouldn't be honest now would it?'

'Well, you have shown yourself to be, how I should put this… capable of deceit.'

I decided to let his less than kind evaluation of me lie.

Tracking down Janelle Chapman wasn't something I thought I would ever need to do, or wanted to for that matter, but sometimes needs must when the devil drives and I needed an expert.

I had erased all traces of Janelle from my life after she stole Roberto from me. I had deleted all of her old emails and blocked her number on my mobile phone. I knew that she had managed to obtain her degree, although quite how she managed that I will never know seeing how she spent every weekend in London with my fiancé. I'd heard from those who had stayed in contact with her that she had moved to Liverpool and was now working in insurance in some capacity or other.

Even though going behind my back with Roberto had ended badly for her, I found what she had done to me impossible to forgive. However, right now I needed to put all that aside when I remembered that Janelle knew an awful lot about Pop and Abstract Art, that was her speciality and she was also familiar with the most prominent artists in that genre. I was also hoping that given her knowledge about the world of insurance she would be able to find out if the photograph we had was really that of a stolen piece of artwork.

I scrolled through the long list of blocked numbers on my phone. Most were of persistent and annoying call centres offering to help me make a claim on a car accident that I'd apparently forgotten I'd had. Janelle's number was at the bottom of the list. I unblocked her and took a photograph of the picture we had discovered in Oliver's bag and texted it to her with a message.

Janelle, is this a stolen painting?
If it is I know where to find it.
Rebecca

Short and sweet. I pressed send and waited for a reply, hoping she hadn't blocked my number too. Alex was experimenting with the laptop I had recovered from Oliver's apartment with about as much luck as I had.

Now I had set the wheels in motion of an idea that was forming in my mind, I realise the whole situation was completely surreal. Oliver has been murdered, Alex was a hunted man and I was planning revenge on one of London's most dangerous criminals. Was this real, how could this possibly be happening?

But then I thought of my beloved dead Poppa and a shudder went down my spine as I imagined what he must have gone through. That only made me more determined. I was not a woman to be messed around, I had already proved that. I wandered over to the kitchen to make coffee and my mobile phone beeped an alert that a text had been received. Could that be

205

Janelle already? My heart was suddenly beating fast with anticipation. It was indeed Janelle.

Hi Rebecca, can I phone you?

I hadn't expected that, well actually I didn't know what to expect so I texted her back.

Yes, call me now

'Alex,' I called. 'It's her, its Janelle. She's going to call me.' We gathered around the dining table and waited for the phone to ring. Maybe Janelle had thought twice about it, or maybe she was gathering up her courage because nothing happened right away.

'What's she waiting for?' I complained and as I did, the phone rang loudly, making us both jump. I answered, pressing the loudspeaker button so that Alex could listen in.

'Hello Janelle?' I asked

'Yes it's me Rebecca. Listen before we go any further I just want to say sorry for you know… what happened. We didn't ever get the chance to talk about it. I was too frightened to admit what I'd done so I …'

I wasn't in the mood to listen to her ramblings so I cut her short. 'It's okay Janelle, a lot of water has flown under the bridge since then maybe it did me a favour in the end. Listen, there's really no need to talk about it. What I need now is your help, that's if you're willing to help me of course?

'Oh yes, of course I want to help. I have to say I was surprised to receive your text but even more surprised to see the picture you sent me. You're not in any trouble are you, do you have the painting?'

'No, of course I'm not in trouble and no I don't have it. As my text said, I know where the painting is. Is it a stolen Janelle?'

'Yes it's a work by Howard Hodgkin that was stolen from a collection in Antwerp four years ago.'

I smiled at Alex who was listening to our conversation intently. 'I thought so, I couldn't tell from the photograph we have and certainly couldn't read the artist's signature but I had a vague recollection I'd seen it before.'

'And you say you know where it is?' Janelle asked. 'Have you been offered it by someone?'

'Nothing like that, I just happen to know whose wall it's hanging on.'

Janelle continued to provide us with more details. 'I checked and found out that the insurers paid out on it so there will be a reward for its recovery. You should let the police know where it is.'

'No, we can't go to the police.'

'Why not?'

'Because we're going to recover it ourselves and I want you to help us.'

There was a short silence until Janelle spoke again. 'You want me to help you recover it?'

'Yes, we need an expert to identify it properly. After all it could be a fake.'

Alex raised an eyebrow at me when I mentioned the word *fake*.

'Will this be dangerous?' asked Janelle.

'No of course it won't be dangerous,' I lied. 'Now will you help me or not?'

'Err, okay,' she promised.

'Good. We are getting a train to Manchester tonight. Can you pick us up from Piccadilly Station?'

'Tonight?'

'Yes tonight. That's not a problem is it? I thought you wanted to help.'

'I do, I do Rebecca. What time?'

'I'll text you later on when you know our arrival time,' and with that I ended the call. When I knew she couldn't hear me anymore I added the closing word. 'Bitch.'

Alex stared at me with eyes wide open.

'What?' I said to him, shrugging my shoulders to show disdain for his unspoken question. Still Alex stared at me so I assumed he actually required an answer. 'When I was at University I was engaged.

'You were engaged?' Alex asked surprised

'Yes, do you want me to tell you the story or not?'

'Sorry.'

I took a deep breath and started again. 'When I was at University I was engaged. Yes, I know I was young but I was,' I added before Alex could interrupt again.

He sat at the table and listened intently as I told him the story of my engagement to Roberto and Janelle's duplicitous actions whilst I was away in Italy studying.

Eventually, my tale of woe finished, Alex sat smiling at me and shaking his head then said, 'If I'd known you could harbour a grudge so long I would never have come back. I'm hoping I'm forgiven now and there isn't any more to come?'

He raised his hand to his face and gently felt the damage I had inflicted to his lip the day before.

'Yes, you're forgiven,' I laughed. 'But let that be a warning to you.'

'Is Janelle forgiven too?'

'She will be if she helps us get our hands on that painting.'

The bright afternoon sun broke through into the room from a break in the clouds forcing Alex to shield his eyes. He rose from the table to adjust the window blinds. 'So apparently we're rushing up to Manchester tonight?'

'There's no time like the present,' I said.

Alex gazed out of the window at the street below, pausing with his adjustment of the blinds slats. 'We may have to put those plans on hold,' he announced gesturing for me to join him at the window. 'Take a look down the street,' he told me. 'Can you see that big red car?

Scanning the road below I spied a large red 4x4 and leaning against it smoking a cigarette was a man I recognised. He was the one who had aimed a kick at Alex whilst he posed as a homeless guy. 'I recognised that car and that man leaning against it,' I told Alex.

'So do I,' he agreed.' It seems like they haven't given up looking for me so they've turned their attention to you in the hope of finding me. I might have known they'd do this.'

'I thought there were two of them?'

'There are. Is there another entrance to this building?'

'Yes, an emergency exit at the rear of the building.' I told him.

Alex angled the slats of the blinds so that it was impossible to see into the window from the street. 'Well, unless we can creep out in disguise, we're going nowhere in a hurry.'

When faced with a dilemma my brain seems to kick in and come up with a solution. Some people might describe this as some sort of survival mechanism, I've heard it called fight-or-flight. But I like to describe it as cunning. I can be as cunning as a fox.

'Can you ride a motorbike?' I asked Alex. 'It will make this easier if you can.'

***

An hour later a food delivery motorcycle and rider pulled up outside the main doors to my building. The helmeted rider dismounted and pressed the intercom to my flat. I buzzed him in. All the two men now sitting in the 4x4 saw was a takeaway meal being delivered, nothing suspicious there.

I knew I could rely on Luigi to get us out of a jam and fortunately he didn't ask too many questions. The tap on the door told us that the delivery guy had reached our floor. Alex opened the door to let him in. When the rider took off his motorcycle helmet I could see it was Andy, one of the kitchen assistants at Luigi's restaurant.

210

Andy was grinning like a Cheshire cat, happy to be part of his scheme.

I never thought I would be so pleased to see a food delivery motorcyclist who had no food in his backpack. 'Hello Andy, you're a lifesaver.'

'Delivery for Miss Harper,' quipped Andy.

'Let's do the swap then you two,' I instructed the men. 'The quicker we do this, the quicker we are out of here.'

Andy flipped off his backpack and took out a denim jacket and a pair of trainers. He slipped off his motorcycle jacket, unlaced his boots and removed them from his feet. Once all of the motorcycling gear was handed to Alex he donned them in minutes and when he finally slipped the crash helmet onto his head nobody would ever know he wasn't the same person who had entered my flat a few moments earlier.

'Now, do you think you can find your way to Luigi's restaurant?' I asked Alex.

'I think so,' he replied. I'll set Google Maps to help me.'

'Good boy, I'll meet you there as soon as I can.'

Andy handed the motorcycle keys over and helped Alex on with the backpack.

'You'll be careful with my bike won't you? I haven't finished paying for it yet.'

I kissed Alex on the lips and flipped the visor over his face and steered him out of the door. Waiting a few minutes for him to reach the street, I watched as Alex disguised as Andy, mounted the bike fired the engine into life and rode away.

All the two men in the red 4x4 saw was a food delivery guy arrive at the building, make his drop off and ride away. Five minutes later they saw a young man in denim jacket leave the building and stride purposely off down the street to the tube station. A further five minutes after Andy had left I stepped out into the street.

Before I left the flat, however, I had placed a small piece of masking tape across the top of the door, out of site. If anyone entered my apartment whilst I was away then the tape would break telling me so.

I paused and looked across to where Robins' men were parked. I noticed how they both slunk down in their seats for fear I would recognise them from the brief confrontation outside Alex's practice. Smiling to myself I thought that they should fear me as after all, I was a fearsome woman. I was smart and they were clearly stupid. They were stupid to be in full view of my apartment window and stupid to be parked across the street, especially during the early evening traffic.

Within a few seconds of me waiting at the kerbside I hailed a cab going in the opposite direction to the way my observer's car was pointed and sped away. From the rear window of the cab I saw them try to break into the endless flow of the traffic, but within a brief moment they disappeared from my view and me from theirs. I did briefly check to see if they had managed to follow me, but they hadn't.

Alex and I met up again at Luigi's as planned after a few hugs, and promises to be careful, we took the District and then the Victoria lines to Euston Station.

CHAPTER 19

We sat opposite each other on the Virgin West Coast train to Manchester. I studied carefully the two tickets I held in my hand. '£310 each, that's ridiculous. I just want to ride on the train not buy the bloody thing.'

'Did we really have to travel first class?' Alex asked, slightly perturbed by my lavish display of spending.

'Yes we do. We need some level of privacy so we can talk about what we're going to do when we get up there. These trains can get pretty full and I didn't want to be sitting in a crowded carriage in economy.'

'Economy... you do know this is a train not an aeroplane don't you?

'You know what I mean,' I replied rolling my eyes at his sarcastic comment. But there again, did he know what I meant? Had I actually explained to Alex the details of my idea for what we would do when we surprised Marcus Pearson? I realised I had also left Janelle dangling, but there again maybe she deserved to be left dangling, I needed her, I wished I didn't but I did. I needed Alex too.

It was almost as if Alex had read my mind and he leaned forward across the table between us. 'So explain to me what your devious little mind is thinking.'

I leaned in towards him so that our faces were just inches apart and whispered 'This is what we're going to do. We go to the Pearson mansion and we take the painting for ourselves, after Janelle has authenticated it for us of course.'

'Don't you think Marcus might object to that?'

'He might, but he's guilty of handling stolen goods and if he's a big a coward as you suggest he is, I'm sure he'll see it our way. Plus, you're going to threaten him.'

'Am I?'

'I thought you might enjoy that?'

'I've seen all the threatening I need to see thank you Rebecca, but what about the stuff he has on me and what I've done?'

Had I taken too much for granted that Alex might want to reap his own revenge in some way by taking it out on the man who had caused him to slip into wrongdoing? Perhaps he had seen enough violence and I was getting carried away. With any luck it wouldn't come to that so I decided to rein my excitement in a little.

'Don't forget Alex that you did manage to retrieve the disc with the video of you on it from Oliver and even if Pearson has a copy what does it prove? Whereas Marcus Pearson has an extremely valuable painting hanging on the wall of his house and that is easy to prove. So easy it could put him behind bars. That's what we'll threaten him with.'

Alex sat back in his seat again. I could tell he was pondering on the details of my plan. After a few minutes he asked, 'Once we have the painting what are we supposed to do with it exactly?'

215

'We reunite it with Robins,' I replied with a smile to reassure Alex that I had everything covered and had considered every eventuality.

Alex looked less than convinced and mumbled to himself, but with enough volume for me to hear. 'I don't get it.'

'You will my darling, believe me you will. That's once I have worked out all of the finer details.'

He folded his arms in disgust and looked out of the window into the darkness which made me wonder if I was really in the dark myself. Was I ignorant of all of the facts, of all of the things that could go wrong? Perhaps I was guilty of not thinking this through fully and the possibility that not everything was going the way I had imagined it would.

I rose from my seat. 'I just going to the loo,' I lied to Alex and made my way along the carriage, steadying myself on the other people's seats as the train raced north at maximum speed. I was in a hurry to set in place another piece of the jigsaw. Once seated on the closed lid of the toilet, where a label listed a number of unthinkable objects that I was forbidden to flush down it, I made a call to my friendly printing expert Phillip. I needed to ask him another favour, this one a little riskier than the last job I had asked him to do for me. Luckily Phillip trusted me and agreed to my request without asking why.

The rest of the journey passed with a certain amount of restless tension between Alex and me. It wasn't because we had somehow fallen out with each other, it was because we were both starting to consider the enormity of what we were about to do.

Would it have been easier for me to send Alex away, or maybe go off with him somewhere far, far away? But then I wouldn't have been satisfied with gaining closure for Poppa's death. For Oliver's death come to that, even though he tried to cheat me. I couldn't help but try and imagining what Alex was thinking. A few short months ago he was a young, aspiring physiotherapist with the whole world before him. Now he was a fugitive, a fraudster, had taken a man's life and all because of Marcus Pearson. What was going through his mind?

***

The train rolled into Manchester Piccadilly just after 10:00pm and as arranged in my texts to Janelle we met at the information point of the station's main concourse. I recognised her immediately as she stood under the information sign waiting to meet us. She hadn't changed that much I thought, except for the fact that she had maybe gained a few pounds, but then again who of us hadn't?

I breathed in as I approached her, buttoning up my jacket and sucking my breath in just in case she was thinking the same about me.

Where do you start with someone you have a history with? What do you say to someone you dislike but need to get along with? I started with a simple, 'Hello Janelle.'

'Hello Rebecca,' was her mirrored reply.

Alex, sensing the tension, stepped forward and reached his hand out to Janelle. 'Hello I'm Alex, pleased to meet you,' he said to break the feeling of unease that existed between us.

To say I was a little miffed with Alex for being so forward would be an understatement. But as I watched Janelle's reaction towards him my fears dissolved into the night air. Her forced smile and the lack of eye contact told me she was not a woman on the prowl.

'My car's in the multi-storey. It's just a short walk,' she informed us and off we strode with Janelle leading the way.

Once outside I drew level with Janelle, despite the Olympian pace she was setting, I asked her what she had learned about the painting's history. Without breaking step, Janelle reached into the cavernous bag over her shoulder and handed me a plastic sleeve containing a sheaf of papers.

'So as I told you on the phone, the painting was stolen from a collector in Antwerp four years ago. The local police believe it was a professional job, stolen to order.'

'Why choose this painting?' I asked. 'Is Howard Hodgkin so famous that someone would order the theft of one of his pieces of work?'

'His work is famous enough in abstract art circles, but maybe not so famous that it would make the headlines and therefore be impossible for the thief to sell. It's also possible it helps that the artist isn't with us anymore.'

'Is an artist only appreciated after he dies?'

'They often are I suppose. Hodgkin's painting was valued at somewhere between one-and-a-half and two-and-a-half million pounds. It was insured for that much and paid out.'

Alex, who had been following slightly behind us, drew level and questioned Janelle on what she had just told me. 'So if I understand this right what you are saying is it isn't worth a thief stealing a really famous painting because it would be all over the news?'

'That's right. Something famous is just impossible to fence. It's not as if a buyer could then go and hang it on their wall.'

'So something a little more obscure is easier to pass on?'

'Yes, it would be. Usually such paintings are stolen so that the thieves use the proceeds to fund some other crime.'

'Like drugs?'

'Possibly.'

Obviously, Janelle had made an impressive effort to find out as much background information as she possibly could to ensure our painting was definitely the one in question. I pulled the documents out of the plastic sleeve as we continued our walk to the car park.

A copy of an article from a fine art magazine carried the story of the theft and the accompanying photograph confirmed it was the same as that discovered in Oliver's briefcase. Of course it still remained to be seen if the artwork we were on our way to investigate was indeed the true original. As we know, fakes and copies really do exist.

Janelle's car was a blue Mini with a white roof. Alex, ever the gentleman, crawled into the back and tried to manoeuvre into a comfortable position. A feat that appeared quite impossible for him and he settled for half lying, half sitting across the entire back seat.

'Do you have the address where we're headed?' asked Janelle.

Alex quoted the postcode to her which she entered into the app on her mobile phone.

We drove in silence as the little Mini navigated the Manchester streets. Soon we were out of the city and heading towards Alderley Edge. After what seemed like an interminable age Janelle broke the nervous quiet in the car.

'I'm glad to help Rebecca, I think I owe you that much, but what exactly are we supposed to be doing. I can't face any more trouble right at this moment,' said Janelle in a subdued tone.

'Listen Janelle,' I replied. 'As I said on the phone, all that is behind us now, it's history and best forgotten. There won't be any trouble from me I can assure you.'

'That's not what I meant,' she continued. 'Things haven't been going so well for me lately and I've had some problems at work. The last thing I need now is for me to be involved in something illegal and lose my job.'

This was no lie; I could sense real sadness in her voice, which to begin with I assumed was her remorse, but there was something else in her voice. Was it fear?

'I'm sorry to hear that Janelle and I don't want you worry that we are up to something illegal because we're not doing anything of the sort.'

Telling her a little white lie wouldn't do her any harm I told myself. While I wasn't quite sure exactly how my scheme was going to pan out I didn't think it would be illegal exactly, but I did know that we should really be telling the police everything we knew and let deal with it.

'I'm sorry you've had some problems,' I added lying again.

'And my husband has left me,' she managed to add with a wavering voice.

'I'm sorry Janelle,'

'Why should you be sorry? Perhaps you think I deserve it?'

'No, I am really sorry because nobody deserves that. Nobody... and that includes you Janelle.' I was really sorry. Now I felt like a real cow.

Sensing that she had been given permission to get things off her chest Janelle started to explain. 'We'd only been married for eighteen months and then a week before my birthday he left me for his ex.'

'Just before your birthday?' Asked Alex, leaning forward from the back of the car to hear to story better.

'Apparently he said he was being kind and didn't want to lead me on.'

'Lead you on? I asked incredulously. 'He'd married you for god's sake. How did he figure he was leading you on?'

'He told me that he had made a mistake when he married me. That he'd done it on the rebound after splitting up with her. He said she was his real love and they were getting back together. My life fell apart and I couldn't face work. I missed appointments, made lots of errors and then I really messed up and did something that cost the firm a lot of money. I almost ended up getting the sack.'

Oh my, now I was really sorry for her because I could obviously see how sad she was. You would not wish that on anyone… and I should know.

I looked over to see a tear rolling down her cheek which she wiped away with her hand. What can you say to a person who has just laid their soul bare to you? I turned round to Alex, with a face that said, *help me out here please!*

'Have you considered hypnotherapy?' Alex asked. 'It can really help to ease your state of mind.'

I made another face to Alex. A face that said, *what the f…*

'It'll be alright Janelle,' I said in my best reassuring tone. 'It's always alright in the end. Just hang on in there.'

We drove on in silence.

Just before midnight we arrived at our destination, Alex directing us passed properties shielded by high, impenetrable walls and hedges to a set of iron gates through which we could see a sweeping gravel drive leading up to an impressive, large house. We parked just outside the gates and the three of us climbed out of the Mini.

Alex looked through the gate to the house he knew so well and I wondered what he was thinking now he was standing outside it again.

'The gates are locked and there's an intercom on the gate posts to ask for access,' he said.

'There's no point in hanging around,' I thought, so striding up to the intercom I pushed the illuminated button and waited. Nothing happened so I pressed it again, for longer this time. A light came on at an upstairs window, urging whoever had turned it on into action. I pressed the button for a third time.

Eventually light flooded the garden from windows surrounding the front door. Someone had clearly descended the stairs to answer my incessant button pressing and a few seconds later the intercom crackled into life and a drowsy sounding voice asked, 'Who is it?'

'Mr. Pearson?' I asked, looking over to Alex for confirmation. He nodded to me.

'Yes, that's me. Who is it?'

'Detective Inspector Smith, Cheshire Police.'

Janelle was shocked and put her hand to her mouth to suppress a gasp.

Alex, equally wide eyed, whispered loudly, 'Are you insane… impersonating a police officer?'

I shrugged my shoulders nonchalantly and turned my attention back to the intercom where the voice asked. 'What is it, is everything alright?'

'Mr. Pearson, we have reason to believe that you are in possession of an extremely valuable stolen painting and we have a warrant to search your property.'

'What do you mean? What stolen painting?'

'Open up Mr. Pearson.'

The voice was getting angrier, if not a little confused, 'I don't have a stolen painting.'

'Mr. Pearson, did you buy a piece of abstract art by Howard Hodgkin from a Mr Oliver Crosby?'

'I've bought several paintings from him, what of it?'

'At least one of those paintings is stolen and if you don't want to be charged with being an accomplice to his crimes you will open this gate and let us investigate.'

The intercom went ominously quiet for a few moments and then with a clunk the gates began to slowly open. To be honest I didn't expect my bluff to work but it did and I hurried Alex and Janelle into the car.

'Quickly, drive up to the house before he changes his mind.'

The pair of them didn't look that thrilled, but did it anyway.

The gravel on the drive crunched under the wheels of the car and as we pulled up level with the door to the house I jumped out as quickly as possible, carried away by the moment and the excitement of what I was doing.

As I reached the door I could hear the clicking of the locks being undone and chains being released. I was poised ready immediately the door opened, thrusting the magazine clipping Janelle had given me about the painting's theft into Marcus Pearson's face. But all of a sudden... wham.

Alex barged right past me, almost knocking me over in the process, to grab Pearson by the collar of his Hugo Boss dressing gown and marched him backwards, at speed, down the hallway.

'What are you doing, you're not the police, get off me,' screamed a terrified Pearson.

They stopped at the end of the large hall, with its splendid double height stairway, to stand in front of a garish painting which seemed out of place in a row of more traditional pieces.

Alex still had hold of a shouting, struggling Pearson but now by the scruff of his neck as he announced. 'Here it is Rebecca, this is it.'

And truly it was.

I held up the photograph Oliver had taken next to it and sure enough they were identical.

'Well, well Mr. Pearson. Who's been a naughty boy then?' I asked.

Pearson was so petrified by our intrusion and Alex's rough treatment that he could only mumble, 'I don't know what you are talking about. I did buy this from Oliver, he told me he was acting on behalf of the owner.'

'Not strictly accurate I'm afraid. Whoever Oliver was working on behalf of certainly wasn't the real owner.'

I handed Pearson the magazine article about the theft, which he tried to read whilst Alex kept a tight grip on him to prevent him fleeing.

'Maybe this is only a copy,' he pleaded in vain.

'I'll bet it was expensive for a copy, but shall we find out?'

Given how Janelle had expressed her own fears about getting into trouble I was pleased to see that she hadn't fled herself and had followed closely behind. Without needing a prompt she carefully studied the modern masterpiece we had come to recover. She turned on all of the hall lights, fully illuminating the room, enabling her to carry out the task she had come to perform.

She carefully studied the painting, standing back to look at the whole effect the artwork gave and at the density of the vibrant colours. Moving in much closer Janelle studied the brushwork, her eyes hovering over the surface.

'Alex, could you help me look at the back of the picture?' She asked.

Letting go of the captive, Alex instructed him, 'Don't move if you know what's good for you.'

Pearson adjusted his dressing gown into a respectable manner. If not putting up at least some sort of a fight wasn't embarrassment enough for him, his man parts had been exposed in full display due to Alex' rough treatment. Alex helped Janelle lift the painting from the wall and she examined the labels stuck on the back, which indicated the history of its ownership.

She checked the details off against a sheet of information she had prepared in advance and ran a finger over a stencilled number she had noticed in one corner.

'This is the real thing,' she announced, holding up the sheet of paper she held in a display of triumph. 'I've been able to verify the previous ownership and there is a stencilled lot number on the back which matches its last auction appearance.'

Marcus Pearson tried to gather himself together but was clearly well and truly terrified by Alex and what he might do.

'You absolute shit of a man,' Alex sneered at him, causing Pearson to shrink back further. 'Bringing a stolen painting into your mother's house and hanging it on the wall for everyone to see. What sort of fucking low-life are you?'

'I didn't know honestly I didn't, I swear it. It was Oliver who persuaded me to buy it, I thought it was legitimate. It's Oliver you need to ask about all this not me. You should be asking him.'

'We would ask, only Oliver's dead,' I informed him.

'What… Oliver's dead. What do you mean dead?' Pearson's trembling voice asked.

'As in murdered,' Alex explained. 'The people he was working for, the same people who acquired the painting you have here, didn't like him anymore or the things he was doing so they beat him up, tied a big heavy block to his feet and threw him in the Thames to drown.'

Janelle gasped for the second time in as many minutes. The colour drained from Pearson's face and he reached out to grab hold of one of the staircase spindles to save himself from falling. A little melodramatic I thought, but he didn't look well, that much I could see.

'I don't understand,' Pearson moaned. 'I don't understand what's going on. I don't know who you people are or what you want from me. I swear I had nothing to do with any of this.'

As Alex had been playing bad cop, I thought I should take a turn now by playing good cop. I took a step towards Pearson and taking his arm gently in my hands I directed him over to a chair to sit on.

'There Marcus, take a few deep breaths and you'll feel fine in a second or two. Now of course you know Alex here don't you?' Marcus acknowledged my question with a nod of his head. 'Well just like you, Alex and I knew Oliver and just like you we also fell victim to his dishonesty. Now the people who murdered poor Oliver need to cover their tracks by finding anyone who had dealings with him.'

'What do you mean?' asked Pearson. 'Am I in danger?'

This is going well I thought, he's asking all of the right questions. 'Yes you are,' I answered gravely.'

'Oh my god,' he groaned, placing his head between his legs to stop himself from fainting.

'And so of course are we,' I waived my arm around the room in a dramatic manner to indicate the three of us standing there with him.

I'm not sure if that was supposed to comfort him or not, but clearly it was of no comfort because he groaned again and placed his head further between his trembling legs.

'Now the only way to prevent this from happening is to take this painting to the police, implicate the murderers in its theft and tell them what they did to your friend Oliver.'

'But surely they don't know anything about me?'

'They will when I tell them,' said Alex

'Take the painting. Take the painting away now, you can have it,'

'This was going better than I could have imagined,' I thought.

I was feeling quite proud of myself that he had caved in so quickly, given that I had no real plan for how I was going to achieve this before we arrived.

'A very wise decision Mr. Pearson, if I may say so. Alex, take the painting down and we'll be on our way.'

Janelle, who had been silent since confirming the painting was an original, unexpectedly became the practical one. 'I think we should protect this painting if we are going to take it with us. Do you still have the shipping crate?'

Pearson shook his head to indicate he didn't.

'We should at least wrap it in a blanket or something. We must take great care. It's worth a great deal of money.'

'How much money?' A suddenly curious Pearson asked.

'At least £2 million.'

Marcus Pearson let out another groan and returned his head between his legs, but unfortunately for him Pearson didn't remain in that position for long.

Yanking the unfortunate man from his chair, Alex announced, 'I know where the blankets are,' grabbing him by the scruff of the neck again and force-marched him up the stairs.

Janelle and I followed close behind, maybe too close as we had to suffer flashes of Pearson's naked back-side as we climbed.

Alex headed for what I guessed was Mrs. Pearson's old bedroom, whilst all along the way her snivelling son pleaded to be let go. When we reached the room we could all see why he didn't want to go in there. Lying face down across the bed, barely covered with a red satin sheet was a naked girl. On the bedside table next to her was a line of white powder and a credit card.

The bedroom had the look and feel of a Parisian brothel, or at least how I imagined such a place would appear. But I was sure this was a style Mrs. Pearson had never contemplated. Frilly velvet lampshade cast a subdued glow against garish flock wallpaper and the bed, with its clichéd satin bed linen. The room looked more 19th century bordello than 21st century Cheshire.

As I went over to check if the girl was breathing Alex tightened his grip on Pearson who was now begging Alex not to hurt him. The girl was breathing but obviously well out of it. I nodded to Alex, gesturing that she was alive at least, but anger was now pursing through the man's vein. An anger the like I had never seen before.

'Look in the bedside table draw,' he growled.

I slid open the top draw to take a peek inside, then slid it fully open so that Alex could see what I had discovered. Lined up neatly were several plastic bags of the white powder, just as I had found in Oliver's apartment.

Alex dragged his prisoner over to a pair of long curtains at the side of the room and drawing them aside revealed a set of French windows leading to a small terrace and balcony. Alex flung the doors open wide and to my horror he forced Pearson's back over the balcony railings and I feared he was going to let him fall. So did Pearson.

'No Alex please, please let me go,' he wailed, begging for his life.

'You disgusting piece of shit,' sneered Alex, his face contorted with sheer revulsion of the man whose life he was holding in his hands.

The violence I saw in Alex's face was terrifying. All of the hate he had held for Marcus Pearson had come to a head. Like a volcano he was ready to blow and I knew I had to intervene quickly before Marcus Pearson actually did fall to his death.

'I'll give you anything. Anything Alex please.' he implored.

I raced out to the terrace and placing my hands on Alex's trembling shoulders I attempted to calm him down. 'Alex, stop. Come on, calm down. Alex, come on now. Let him go. Let him go.'

Slowly Alex pulled the struggling man from the edge of the balcony and dropped him to the floor. Pearson lay on the terrace, crying with relief that he wasn't about to fall to his death. Silently Alex stepped back into the bedroom, walked over to the bed and scooped up the bags of white powder then over to a cupboard, and took out a large sky blue woollen blanket.

In the meantime Janelle had placed the unconscious girl in the recovery position and covered her with the sheet. None of us spoke as Alex led the way downstairs and Pearson's sobs became fainter. Alex wrapped the painting as best he could with the blanket and carried it outside to the car.

As we followed behind Janelle placed her hand on my arm. 'Rebecca, there is a sizable reward for the recovery of this painting, and not that I want it for myself, but if I were to let my employer know that we have it back safe and sound then I know it would help me out a lot.'

I hadn't expected that from her. I knew Janelle had been an unwilling accomplice since we met at the railway station and the fracas she had witnessed in the house surely couldn't have done anything to encourage her. But here she was asking me to practically hand over the painting to her. I had to admire her temerity.

'Look Janelle,' I answered. 'I am so grateful that you helped us out but Alex and I really need the painting. He wasn't lying when Alex told Marcus that we are in danger. Alex witnessed a murder and now those that did it are looking for him. This painting may be the only thing that protects us.'

Janelle looked downhearted and after what she had done to help us I really did feel sorry for her. Maybe I did owe her, after all and she had been through quite a lot recently. Getting my revenge didn't seem appropriate now.

'This is what I can do for you. We aren't planning to keep the painting for ourselves, you know that. But you could do us one more favour.'

Janelle raised her eyebrows in anticipation.

'At some point we will need someone to tip off the police for us and if that person is you, well then perhaps you could get the credit?'

'Okay, but I don't want to put myself in any danger and like I said… I don't need any more trouble either.'

'No you won't be in any danger and you don't need to come with us. When we need you to make the call I'll send you a text and tell you what to say.'

I could see Janelle was mulling that over in her head and after a few moments agreed.

'I can do that, if you promise not to forget me. I really need this Rebecca.'

We caught up with Alex who was trying to load the painting in to the Mini.

'The bloody thing is too big to get in the car,' he complained. 'I've tried every angle and including the tailgate and it won't go in.'

'Hmm, just wait here,' I told them and went back inside the house.

I went back upstairs to where I could hear Pearson still sobbing, although a little softer now. Almost like a little baby at the end of a long blub-session.

He looked up when he saw me enter the room and wiped his face along the arm of his dressing gown sleeve.

'Mr. Pearson. If you really do value your life the first thing you are going to do is phone an ambulance for this poor girl. Then you're going to do something for me that will help me to prevent Alex visiting you again. I don't think he likes you.'

Pearson's tear stained face looked up at me pathetically. He nodded in agreement to indicate he was willing.

'Do you remember that you told Alex you would give him anything if he didn't hurt you?'

Back outside at the car Janelle and Alex were still struggling with the impossible.

"Will these help?' I asked Alex, holding up a set of keys in front of him. 'Marcus has generously offered to lend us his Range Rover.'

I handed the keys to him and turned to Janelle.

'Thanks so much for your help Janelle, we really appreciated it. Now remember, I'll text you when it's time for your help again, okay?'

'Okay,' she replied simply, climbed in her blue Mini and drove away.

I guess it was too much to expect a hug but there was not even a shake of hands. How rude.

By now Alex had stowed the painting safely in the Pearson Range Rover and was waiting in the driving seat with the engine running.

'Aren't you going to see if you get a refund on the unused return train tickets?' he asked sarcastically.

I smiled back at him. My Alex had returned from the edge of his darkness.

CHAPTER 20

We arrived back in London in the early hours of the morning and parking up in the underground carpark of my building. Doing so certainly helped us unload the painting away from prying eyes. At four in the morning not a soul was up and about to see us bundle the blanket wrapped painting into the lift to ascend up to my floor.

Keeping as quiet as church mice, because who wouldn't want to be quiet carrying a stolen painting around before dawn, we set it down outside the door to the apartment so that I could retrieve the door key from the bottom of my bag.

Just before opening the door I looked up into the corner of the door frame to see if the tape was still in place… it was torn in two.

'Alex look, the tape's broken,' I said, pointing up to the top of the door where the ragged ends of two halves of tape gave evidence that someone had entered the apartment.

'Give me the key and wait here,' Alex told me whilst he gingerly unlocked the door, opening it as silently as he could.'

I certainly wasn't waiting outside if someone was in my apartment and followed closely behind despite his instruction. Sensing that I hadn't obeyed his command, Alex gave me a stern look but it was too late now. This was my apartment and if someone was inside I wanted to know. However, I did stay close to the door in case a hasty retreat was called for, realising that I may not be as brave as I had been telling myself lately.

Alex moved about in silence, opening the doors to each room and peering inside. 'There's no one inside now,' he confirmed

I breathed a sigh of relief and brought the painting in from the corridor, double locking the door and putting the security chain in place. If someone had been in my apartment while we were up north, who were they and what could they have possibly been looking for I wondered?

Alex was obviously thinking the same thing and suggested I take a look around to see if anything of value was missing. Things like jewellery or my laptop because, as Alex explained, it would be better to have been burgled than to have Robins' men targeting me. I searched every room and I could see that nothing of value was missing. Everything was as I had left it, but then Alex made a discovery.

'Rebecca, come in here a minute,' he called from the bedroom. 'Look at this.'

I walked into the room and round to Alex's side of the bed where he stood pointing like those men you see in mail order catalogues. 'What am I looking at? I asked bemused.

'There, look,' he answered sharply still pointing, as though I was some sort of idiot who couldn't see the blindingly obvious.

'What am I looking at?' I asked as if to confirm my stupidity

Alex rolled his eyes and stiffened his arm which was now also shaking slightly as it pointed at the chest of drawers, such was his frustration.

'The drawer… the second one down. There's a sock poking out of it.'

'Now call me stupid if you want Alex,' I thought, 'but I don't think that a sock poking out of a drawer warrants as much drama as being broken in to.'

Alex could see that I still hadn't understood what all the pointing and eye rolling was supposed to be about.

'Someone has been going through the drawers,' he explained and as he did so, opened the drawer with the errant sock poking out of it. 'There, I knew it. Whoever came in here didn't come to steal anything; they came to see if I was holed up in your flat. See how untidy the draw is?'

I stood closer and sure enough the clothes I had laid out so carefully in the draw for Alex to use had been disturbed and his things were lying in a crumpled mess.

'Maybe it was thieves looking for money or something and left when they couldn't find any,' I said unconvincingly.

'Look in your own drawer,' suggested Alex. 'If that's the case, they would have looked in every draw and messed up the lot.'

I knew it was pointless because I knew what I would find. Sure enough, all of the clothes in my own drawers lay flat and undisturbed.

'Robins knows that I'm with you Rebecca,' said Alex. 'Neither of us is safe here anymore.'

***

Within a short time we had each packed a bag with enough things for a few days away. Then we carried the painting back down to the car and drove out into London's early morning traffic, which was already busy. We were alert to any vehicle that looked like the big red 4x4 that Robins' men drove around in. I kept looking over my shoulder, unsure if Alex would be able to spot them in the rear view mirror as he drove.

'Stop doing that,' he chided me each time I turned around in my seat. 'They're not following us.'

It was okay for him to say that I thought, but the knowledge that they had been in my flat and that these same men had also murdered Oliver, sent a shiver down my spine. So much so that I was convinced we were actually being followed.

We drove to Oliver's flat at Greenwich, figuring it was a safe place to hide out. But it was clear to us that we couldn't stay there forever. For one thing Robins knew where I worked and now he also knew that I was harbouring Alex, it was only a matter of time before his thugs caught up with us. Alex and I needed to act and we needed to act fast.

Tidying Oliver's untidy apartment was the first thing on the agenda, we needed a clean space to plan our next move. We also needed food as we realised we hadn't eaten in a long time.

Whilst Alex disposed of bags of rubbish which littered the apartment, I went out to Tesco Express to buy us some breakfast. I was wary about being outside on my own, even though I did agree with Alex that they wouldn't think of looking for us at Oliver's apartment. Nevertheless I couldn't get it out of my head that I was being followed. I couldn't explain it but it was a real feeling. On my way to the supermarket, I kept looking over my shoulder.

There was a great feeling of relief when I made it back to the apartment. Alex had made it look clean and tidy; he clearly was a girls dream, well this girl at least. I made us a breakfast of bacon and eggs and brewed us a large pot of strong coffee. We hadn't slept in 24 hours so we needed a huge caffeine boost to keep us going. As we ate our breakfast and drank our coffee, we discussed our plan of action and how we were going to accomplish it.

First off though, I told Alex that I needed to collect some items that Phillip had prepared for me. It seemed a good idea not to take the car but to blend in with the crowds using public transport. As Robin's men used the roads and a brightly coloured 4 x 4 we decided to do the opposite and use the underground or public transport as much as possible. That way we would know if anyone was following us.

We walked towards the station and I still couldn't shake off the feeling that we were being followed. Looking over my shoulder for the hundredth time, checking for a big red car, I spotted a big red bus instead approaching just yards behind.

'Quick Alex, run' I shouted. 'Let's get the bus, Quick.'

We ran to the bus stop and managed to make it in time. The doors closed behind us and we dropped into the nearest seats, panting for breath.

'What was all that about' asked Alex, once he had recovered his breath.

'To shake off any follower of course' I replied smiling back at him, proud at my cunning. Alex just shook his head in disbelief but I knew what I felt and I wasn't about to take any unnecessary extra risks.

At Greenwich North underground station I stood back from the doors when the train arrived at the platform, only rushing to board just as the doors were closing. I did the same when we changed lines at London Bridge. By now Alex had stopped asking me what the hell I was playing at. He just accepted I was paranoid.

Philip's workshop was in a backstreet, so it was easy to see if we were being followed. He took us to his office and closed the door so that we wouldn't be overheard. It is not every day he had a client asking him to do something highly illegal, so it was a good idea that his staff didn't hear our conversation.

'I trust you Rebecca' said Philip 'And I'm sure you have a very good reason why you asked me to do this.'

Alex looked quite perplexed as I hadn't told him what Philip was printing for me. Taking a key out of his trouser pocket, Philip opened a draw in his desk and took out a shoe-box which he set down in front of me.

'I had to work all night on that,' he said. 'Obviously I had to do it when everyone else had gone home.'

I reached out and pulled the box towards me.

'Philip you really are a good friend and I don't want you to worry about a thing, these will be used with the best of intentions.'

I took the lid off the box and took one of the small bundles out to inspect them, a neatly bound stack of £50 notes. There were twenty bundles in all, a total of £100,000. Of course none were real.

Alex eye's nearly bulged out of his head 'What the hell!' he spluttered.

'I love shoe boxes and what we find in them' I said. 'A lovely piece of work Philip'

'Thank you Rebecca. I try my best.'

Alex had just about recovered his senses and managed to ask, 'What are you going to do with these. Don't you think we are in enough trouble already?'

'I'm going to present these to Mr Robins, as if he is not in enough trouble already.'

I thanked Philip for this hard work and placed the shoebox and its contents into an anonymous looking plastic carrier bag. We made our way back to Greenwich the same way we had come, using the same precautionary measures. This time Alex was more than happy to play along.

It was late afternoon when we got back to the apartment. Tiredness had caught up with us both and we realised that with so much at risk and needing all of our strength for later that night.

We drew all the curtains and snuggled into bed together. Sleep came easy to us both but my dreams were harrowing and bizarre. I dreamt about my Poppa and he was urging me to come with him to seek revenge, although in my dream it wasn't clear what the revenge was for. But I remember him being angry and shouting, which wasn't like the father I knew. For some strange reason we were carrying swords as a weapon and we strode off together to meet our adversaries shouting defiance.

But when we met our enemies we were unable to lift our swords, which had become too heavy. I started shouting for help as a gang of shouting men advanced towards us, afraid of meeting my end and that's when Alex woke me.

The pair of us dressed in the darkest clothes we had as night had fallen outside. We assembled everything we needed for our expedition and placed them by the door ready to leave. But first we needed to prepare Oliver's flat. Alex removed most of the cocaine from Oliver's bedside drawer leaving a single bag to be discovered later. We placed the laptop on the dining table making it easy to find and for good measure we also placed a couple of bundles of the forged money next to it. Then it was time to go.

The marina where Robin's boat was moored wasn't too far from Greenwich but on the north bank of the Thames. It only took us 15 minutes to drive there. As we hoped the place was deserted, there were no cars in the carpark and no lights on in any of the adjacent buildings.

Access to the lines of boats was via gated walkways that required either a PIN number or an access card. Alex, ever the resourceful one, had bought with him the bath-mats from Oliver's apartment. Throwing them over the high fence with lethal looking sharp points at the top, Alex used the mats as protection as he scaled the fence and dropped to the other side. He then opened the gate from the inside and we wedged it open with a concrete block so that we could take the painting and our other gifts for Robin through and along the jetty to his boat.

I was surprised how easy it was to access Robin's boat. The seating area at the rear was just open to the elements inviting me to step aboard, so I did. As I have mentioned before, Alex was a man of many talents and after about 2 minutes of trying to, he defeated the lock on the door of the salon. I helped him carry the painting inside.

Alex looked around for a suitable position, aware that the Hodgkin was a decent size and removed a tasteless, amateur daubing of a sailing ship from the wall, mounting Hodgkin in its place.

'There we are,' Alex announced, standing back and admiring his handiwork. 'Out of sight, in plain view.'

The next task was to hide the other gifts we had for Robins well out of site on the boat. These could be discovered later. Call them surprise presents for him if you will. Alex thought the best place for them would be in the bedroom.

We placed ten bags of cocaine in a drawer next to the bed and the remaining quantity of the forged money in the bottom of the wardrobe.

Alex smiled at me, he really did look like he was enjoying himself and to be honest so was I. If only my heart wasn't beating so fast but I guess that was down to the large amounts of adrenalin pursing through my veins.

Our work completed, it was time to leave. As much as this was exciting, it was dangerous and clearly we were still in danger.

Alex thought the same thing. 'Come on, let's get going and make a few phone calls,' he whispered

Making sure everything in the boat looked undisturbed, we closed the doors to the boat and Alex bought the tasteless painting he had removed from the wall inside the boats salon so we could dispose of it.

'Nobody is going to miss this' he said as he slid the painting off the side of the boat into the blackness of the water.

'I think that's the best place for you, don't you?'
I agree 'Sleeping with the fishes.'

Then I realised what I had said stepping back
from the edge of the boat, I brought my hands to
my face and a horrid cold chill ran through me as
I remembered Oliver's body was also down
there.

Alex sensed my unease and guessed what I
was thinking. After a few seconds pause he said
gently. 'Come on, let's go now.'

Clambering over the side of the boat onto the
jetty, Alex holding my hand as I did so, we were
startled by the voice out of the darkness.

'Well, well, well. So here you are. I knew I'd
find you two eventually.'

As my eyes grew accustomed to the darkness I
could see that the voice belonged to one of the
men I had seen watching my apartment, the man
who had tried to kick Alex in the shop doorway.
He held a gun in his hand and he was pointing it
at us.

'What have you been up to on Mr. Robins'
boat?' He asked threateningly.

Neither of us spoke, I was too frightened to
speak. I'd never seen a gun before let alone have
one pointed at me.

Alex stepped in front of me protectively. 'Put
the gun down, there's no need for that,' he said
bravely.

'Shut up,' snapped the man. 'And stand where
I can see you both,' he ordered.

I came out from my hiding place behind Alex and he reached for my hand, holding mine tightly in his.

'Put your hands where I can see them,' the man commanded us.

I squeezed Alex's hand tighter. I couldn't bring myself to let go of his hand and the little safety holding on to him gave me. Alex raised my hand with his and put up his free hand displaying the palm of it to the grinning brute. I copy Alex, also raising my spare hand. We were helpless.

The brute laughed at us. 'Ah look at them,' he scoffed. 'Is that how you both want to go… holding each other's hands?'

'Do you think your aim is good enough?' Alex asks calmly. 'You tried to shoot me before and yet here I am still.'

The smile disappeared from the man's face. 'I can't miss from this range. I shoot her first then I'll shoot you, but not until you watched her die in front of your eyes. Then you can both go and join your friend.'

He gestured with a flick of his gun to the murky water that was Oliver's grave. The man's arm straightened, pointing directly at me. I swallowed hard.

'I don't suppose if I said the old trick, *"look out… behind you,"* you'd actually turn around to look would you?' I managed to ask him.

He laughed at my question. 'No I wouldn't.'

'Pity,' I said.

The metal pole cracked against the right side of the man's head with such force I actually winced when I heard the sound of metal against skull.

Janelle's aim was firm and true. She dropped the fence pole she had stuck him with onto the decking where it fell with a clatter. Robins' thug lay unconscious next to it.

'My god, what the hell, where'd you come from,' I stuttered, almost incoherently.

'I've been following you,' explained Janelle, 'then I saw this guy was as well.'

She looked down at the body lying motionless on the jetty. Alex had already picked up the gun that lay where the thug had dropped it when the fence pole hit him and knelt over the body.'

'He'll live,' Alex told us.

'You've been following us… what the hell for?' I asked Janelle in disbelief.

'I didn't trust you'd keep your promise to me. I mean, why should you?'

'Because I said I would,' I answered, 'but wow, I'm pleased you didn't trust me. Am I glad to see you?'

Janelle beamed the biggest smile, the first time I had seen her face display happiness since we had met up again in Manchester.

'When you drove away in the Range Rover you borrowed that night, I followed you at a safe distance all the way down to London. I was surprised you didn't notice me to be honest. God girl, you were so difficult to keep tabs on.'

'I knew I was being followed. I could feel it.' I said.

'Well you never saw me and did I lose you more than once. The first time was when you jumped on that bus on the way to the tube station, but I guessed where you were going and I just managed to catch up with you there, despite you jumping through the train doors at the last minute. Then I lost you again on your return journey, the platforms were just too busy by then with all of the commuters heading home.'

'So how is it you're here now?' I asked her, still confused at what had just taken place.

'I knew where you were living and what car you were driving so I bought a GPS tracker and stuck it to the underside of the Range Rover. And I also knew you wouldn't be able to carry the painting on the underground so it was just a case of waiting until you eventually drove somewhere.'

I was astounded at Janelle's ingenuity, or was she just displaying her devious side again I wondered, but then I checked that thought as being utterly disingenuous considering the circumstances. 'Where on earth do you get a GPS tracker from?' I asked her.

'You can buy anything in London if you know where to look,' she answered with a wink. 'Then when you left the apartment building to come here this evening, I was keeping a reasonable distance between us but I couldn't help but notice a big red 4x4 that was always in front of me following you. I could have saved my money on the tracker; you were both easy to follow.'

Janelle looked at the man lying on the ground who was starting to moan a little. Alex had found a bucket on a nearby boat and had filled it with water from over the side of the jetty. He emptied it, unceremoniously, over the man's head. He spluttered and coughed and groggily tried to sit up. Alex helped him by grabbing hold of the back of his collar. A second bucket of cold water helped him recover a little more.

When Alex was sure he was well enough he yanked the man to his feet and walked him over the edge of the jetty and held the gun to the back of his head.

'I don't think I can miss from this range do you? Alex snarled at the man.

'Alex no, you can't,' I pleaded.

Once again I saw the anger that had welled up inside Alex, in the same way he had held Marcus Pearson over the edge of the balcony, the red mist had filled Alex' eyes. The way he spoke through gritted teeth was frightening to hear. He held the man teetering on the edge of the jetty, daring him to speak but he was unable to do so. He could only pant in fear of his impending death.

I froze with fear of my own. Should I move toward Alex and calm him? Should I run towards him to try to knock the gun from his hand?

Alex was too quick for me, with a push of his hand into the frightened man's back, Alex shoved him tumbling into the water. As the man's head resurfaced Alex squatted down to speak to him.

'It isn't very nice being pushed in the back is it?' Alex asked the gasping man. 'Now swim over there.' Alex gestured with the gun over to the far side of the marina.

I looked over to where Alex was pointing and it did look a very long way for a fit person to swim, let alone this rather chubby brute who had only partially recovered from the blow to his head.

'It's too far,' protested the chubby brute.

'You have two choices,' explained Alex. 'In a few minutes the police will be here and you can tell them why you have a gun and why there is the body of a man with a weight tied round his ankles underneath you. Or you can take your chances and start swimming. Oh and by the way, I am going to count to ten and if you haven't made your mind up by then, I'll shoot you.'

'What… no, no wait,' the now terrified thug stammered.

'One… two…'

Alex never got to three, the man started to swim. Not very well it must be said, but he swam as best he could and within a few minutes we lost sight of him in the dark of the night.

''What the hell is all this about you two,' Janelle asked.

'It's a long story,' I answered. 'When we've got several hours to spare I'll explain everything to you.'

We were brought back to reality by Alex.

'Janelle, you really are a life saver and I don't know how to thank you but let's not hang about here, we don't know he hasn't alerted Robins. Let's get going.'

He wiped the gun down, removing his own figure prints and left it on the edge of the jetty to be easily found. The fence pole he threw into the water.

'Now if it's okay with you Janelle,' Alex continued saying. 'Rebecca and I will disappear for a while. Will you be okay phoning the police now?'

'Absolutely, no problem,' she agreed.

'Maybe you could tell the police you've heard gunshots and seen men on the boats and explain your presence here that you've had some sort of tipoff that a valuable stolen painting can be found on Robins' boat. You can tell them that your tipoff also says there's drugs involved too if you like.'

'Leave it to me,' she said. Then turning to me, Janelle held out her hand. 'We're even now? She asked me.

I didn't shake the hand she offered, I walked toward her and wrapped her in my arms.

'We're more than even Janelle.'

Alex and I climbed into the Range Rover and waved to Janelle who was now sitting in her car. She already had a mobile phone to her ears as she waved back to us.

We drove back to my apartment in total amazement, thinking about the events that had just happened. We had only driven a few miles when a number of police cars passed us sirens blaring, lights flashing, going hell for leather in the direction of the mariner. We smiled knowingly at each other.

ONE MONTH LATER

Alex and I sat side by side in the Tuscan sun and gazing down on the beauty of the green landscape, rolling hills and the elegance of rows of cypress trees.

'This is that favourite place in nature that I pictured in my mind when you hypnotised me,' I said.

'When I tried to hypnotise you don't you mean?' replied Alex.

It had been an eventful month following our night at the marina. The plan that Alex and I had cooked up together, although quite sketchy in its conception, worked out better than we could ever have expected despite the small intervention of the man with a gun. We never did find out if he managed to swim all the way to the other side.

On Janelle's tip off the police raided Robins' boat and found the stolen painting, of course with Janelle pointing it out to them.

Sniffer dogs easily located the cocaine Oliver had planted and although we might be criticized for framing Robins with drugs we had discovered elsewhere, it did encourage the authorities to investigate further which unearthed his drugs network and a lot more arrests.

Poor Oliver's body was found by divers looking at the hull of Robins' boat for other evidence of smuggling. When they broke down the door to his apartment police investigators found drugs and the forged £50 notes, both identical to those hidden on Robins' boat. These items tied Oliver to Robins and finding Oliver's laptop where we had conveniently left it, experts were able to bypass the password and found a veritable Aladdin's cave of information. Information on art thefts, where paintings were now and who had them, details of money laundering and all other sorts of criminal activity Robins was involved in.

The strange thing about that was whilst Oliver was not the best at housekeeping in his apartment, or his private life for that matter, he was extremely diligent and organised with his electronic filing system.

Needless to say Robins and a number of his cronies where charged with multiple crimes, including the murder of Oliver. The court case starts in a few months' time and he isn't expected to be free from custody for a very, very long time.

As for Janelle, she decided not to save her career in insurance by sharing the recovery of the stolen painting with her employer. Instead to quit her job and received a nice reward from the paintings insurers that should enable her to move on with her life and make a new start elsewhere.

It was so blissful to lie here in the Italian sun with my gorgeous Alex. I turned to him as he lay there enjoying the peace of the countryside I had known so well from the many family holidays I had enjoyed there. 'Penny for your thoughts?' I asked him.

'I was just thinking about everything we went through just for some old drawing on a yellowing piece of paper. If I never see one of those it will be too soon,' he reflected.

I reached under my lounger and pulled out a small portfolio case I had bought with me. I unzipped it and opening out for him to inspect I asked him, 'Well I don't suppose you're interested in these other two then?

WHAT'S NEXT?

Gio had worked out a great idea for another story we had made a draft for a follow novel which tells more of the story of Janelle and what she did with the reward she received for her part in the recovery of the stolen painting. *'So You're The Other Woman?'* continues the adventure. If you think it's a good idea I carry on our work I would love to hear from you. And if you are interested in being kept up to date with news of the next book and release date etc. keep in contact with us below and I'll add you to the mailing list.

You can follow me on my blog: www.hike-it.org

Or email: -
mailto:gioandkengregory@gmail.com

ABOUT THE AUTHORS

Giuseppina 'Gio' Gregory was a freelance writer born in Italy, but moved to Coventry, England when just 6 years old. Gio trained as a Business Coach and a Hypnotherapist and studied Art History as a mature student at Coventry University. She was never one to stop learning new things.

Ken Gregory is a Chartered Engineer who began his love of writing by producing short stories and scripts for Amateur Dramatics.

Gio and Ken first met in 1974 as volunteers for the Coventry Hospitals Broadcasting Service at the Walsgrave Hospital in Coventry.

Printed in Great Britain
by Amazon

60725864R00156